CHAPTER 1 – LET'S GET THIS PARTY STARTED

The day is September 17th, 2011. A Heavy Metal concert is going on in Austin Texas. In the crowd we find two young lovers. Chris and Cimber. Chris is about five/seven ft. tall with short blond hair about down to his cheeks; he's got a good built body for his size and very blue eyes and is eighteen years old, weighs one hundred fifty two pounds. His girlfriend Cimber very slim and skinny about five/five ft. tall and weighs one hundred twenty pounds. She's got long blond hair and blue eyes, age seventeen years old. They have a goal ahead of them that will change their lives completely. As we now follow them to find out what it is.

"Chris! Chris! Where are you?" yells Cimber lost in the crowd.

"I'm right here babe!"

A hand reaches threw the crowed of people as Cimber grabs it and is pulled to Chris.

"Baby are you okay?" Chris said laughing.

"Yea I'm fine I just got scared for a sec."

"Well alright," said Chris laughing.

"Well the concert is almost over just this last song left baby, you want to head out a bit early to beat the crowd?" Chris asked.

"Yea that sounds great" said Cimber.

They make their way through the crowd and when they get to the back a drunken guy comes up to Cimber and reaches his hand down her pants. Cimber grabbed his hand and immediately pulled it out then slapped the guy.

"I'm going to kick your ass!" yelled Chris.

"Baby he's just drunk." said Cimber.

"BITCH!" yelled the guy at Cimber for slapping him.

"Ok that tears it," said Chris.

He punched the guy in the face and broke his nose.

"Ok dick." says the guy as he begins to swing his fist at Chris.

Chris dipped under him and threw the guy over his shoulders. The guy fell on his back and lay there on the ground gasping for air. Chris walked over and dropped his knee on the guys face then got back up.

"Baby let's go!" said Cimber.

She grabbed Chris's arm and pulled him away.

"Come on baby," she said to him as they walked towards the gate.

After leaving out the gate, they got to their car and headed home.

Chapter 2 — The Recruiter

The next morning was school.

"Fuck today is Monday!" yelled Chris.

"I know baby we got school so get up and get ready baby," said Cimber.

Chris and Cimber had just moved in together last month when he turned eighteen.

"Babe did you get your book?" Cimber said as they walked out the door.

"Yea I almost forgot it but didn't," said Chris smiling at Cimber.

They got in the car and headed to school.

On the way Chris put on a song that he liked to get him pumped for school.

"Awe!" said Cimber as she changed it.

"What the hell babe?" said Chris.

"What?" said Cimber?

"Why did you change it...?" Chris said.

"Because I don't like to listen to heavy stuff in the morning... I want to relax so I am not to hyper in class." Cimber replied.

"Well then why the fuck are you drinking an energy drink...?" said Chris with a confused look on his face.

"Because I want to be awake babe!" said Cimber.

"See I drink just this but don't listen to heavy music so I'm awake but not hyper. If I do both then I'm hyper, but if I just do one I'm awake but not hyper." said Cimber.

"That makes no sense..." said Chris.

"O shut up and just listen to the music I chose!" said Cimber as she turns up the volume.

They arrive at school and as soon as they did the bell rang.

"Oh my god we are late!" said Cimber.

"Damn!" exclaimed Chris.

They ran to class, luckily they had the same classes. They came flying in the door and the teacher Mrs. Turner looked at them along with the rest of the class.

"AH Chris and Cimber, late again…" she said staring at them with an evil look on her face.

"Sor"-"Ah!" the teacher stopped Cimber before she could finish.

"I don't want no more apologies… the both of you will serve Detention at lunch… But on the bright side, yawl made it just in time to answer the question I just asked. And if you answer it correctly I'll excuse you're tardy," said Mrs. Turner.

"And that question is…?" said Chris.

"What is the Capital of Brazil?" asked Mrs. Turner

"Fuck…"said Chris.

"Excuse me Chris?" said Mrs. Turner.

"Nothing mam…" he said looking down at the ground.

"I'll consider that your answer," said Mrs. Turner. "Now go sit down you two… and "Fuck" is not the capital of Brazil."

"The class laughed."

They made their way to their seats and sat next to each other.

...Later on lunch time came around. After they had gotten their food they sat down at the lunch table with their friends.

"Who is that guy in the military uniform?" said Cimber to their friends at the table the sat at.

"He's a Recruiter," said one of the kids named Kevin.

"Yea," said another kid named Paula. "He's here trying to find the best of the best. He's not just recruiting anyone."

"So has like a special forces guy?" Cimber asked.

"Yea!" replied Paula.

Later on Cimber and Chris parted as they had their final classes. The last class they did not have together. She had athletics and he had weight room. They parted and went to their class. Later on in the weight room Chris was lifting as usual. The weight coach stood beside him clocking him.

"Damn Chris!" said Coach Wesley. "You manage to lift four

times your own weight every time. I don't know how a kid your size does it."

As he lifted the recruiter stood in the corner unknowingly watching.

"How does he do on the track?" said the recruiter as he walked up to the coach.

"Well he does tremendous their too." he said to him.

"I want to see It." said the recruiter.

They took Chris out to the track. Cimber was there as well running for her athletics class.

"Ok Chris, I want you to run down there to the yellow line then run back." said the coach.

"Yes sir!" Chris replied.

"Ready... Go!" said the Coach.

Chris ran as fast as he could to the yellow line then ran back. People stopped and watched as they couldn't believe how fast he ran. He finally came back and reached the coach.

"TIME!" Coach yelled.

The Coach showed the stop watch to the Recruiter.

"Twenty seconds in two hundred meters, that's very impressive," said the recruiter.

He then glimpsed over at Cimber who was being clocked as well.

"What is her time?" asked the recruiter as he walked over to the female coach instructing women's athletics.

"21:50 in two hundred meters" she said to him.

He looked at Cimber and Chris.

"You two-come with me," He said.

They followed him into a private room. He shut the door and asked them to have a seat.

"You too have amazing almost super human abilities. I need you two to join the Special Forces." the recruiter said.

"Why?" said Chris.

"Because we need people like you. It will be a great experience and we will pay for your college," said the recruiter.

"I don't see how that's any different from military privileges..." said Chris.

"We will pay you," said the recruiter.

"How much?" asked Cimber.

"$500,000 each," he said.

"Wow when do-we start?" asked Chris.

"Right now," the recruiter said.

"Um… ok sir," said Cimber.

"Please follow me outside," said the recruiter.

They followed him and he led them to a helicopter in the back of the school that was parked in the parking lot where they had reserved parking.

"No wonder there was more cars in student parking today," said Cimber.

They got in the helicopter and they began to take off.

"My mom said I shouldn't even get in a strangers helicopter…" said Cimber.

"Really…? She said that?" asked Chris.

"No" said Cimber "But she said don't get in a strangers car."

"He's a military Recruiter…" said Chris.

"Oh yea!" said Cimber.

Chapter 3 — General Patten and What is

going on

After 3 hours of flying they arrived at a base camp in Arizona.

"We are here," said the recruiter.

"What?" said Cimber as she woke up from sleeping on Chris's lap.

"We are here at the Arizona base camp," said the recruiter.

"Jesus..." said Cimber.

They got out and fallowed him into the building. When they got inside they went down a few hallways and went through a couple of double doors and arrived in a room that looked like a meeting hall with a bunch of people in it, and had a front stage with a projection screen at the back of the stage.

"Find a seat anywhere," said the recruiter to them.

They sat down near the back of the room. Chris and Cimber looked around and noticed there was allot of people in there like them. They looked like they have never been in the military before...all but a few of them. A few had on Military uniforms.

"Ok boys and girls," said a voice.

A man walked up on the stage. He was a big man about six/two feet tall, looks like he is middle aged and was very buff, like he was a body builder... and he had scars on his face.

"I am General Patten," he said. "I'm sure you are all wondering why you are all here...? Well you have been called because you were chosen as the best of the best." He said as he began his speech. "You see we need people who can door more than the average person."

"Why didn't you just get soldiers?" said a random person.

"YOU WILL SHUT YOUR MOUTH WHEN I TALK!" yelled General Patten. "We did not recruit regular military because we do not pay them and allot of them are regular people who want to fight for their country. We had to pay you all to come. Now some of you pussy's will leave after this because your too damn scared to deal with what your about to see. Slide show please!" said General Patten. "Now this is an uncharted island in between the united states and Europe. This island was discovered to be used as a Nuclear weapon base close to Iraq. So we could nuke the fuckers if we had to... The island is named Demo."

He clicked the button on the remote in his hand and a picture of the island came up on the projector screen.

"Now three days ago, a hell hole opened up on this island."

Everyone looked at the General like he was crazy. Then a picture of it appeared on the slide show. As it showed allot of the people in the room began to look worried.

"This hell hole that you see has demons that come out of it at night. Unfortunately the soldier that took this picture was killed and his camera with these pictures was found on the beach," the General continued.

He clicked another button and pictures taken of some of the

Demons came up on the screen.

"Holy shit…" whispered Chris to Cimber.

Cimber grabbed hold of him.

"This island…" the General began to continue.

As he went on Chris looked over to the other side of the room and noticed a girl staring at him. She had long wavy dirty blond hair. And beautiful green eyes. She was very slim, and she was sixteen years old. He smiled at her then she looked back at the screen then so did he. They paid their attention back to the general.

"Now those of you who are scared shitless and want your mommies please leave now so I don't waste anymore of your time," said General Patten.

Five of the kids got up and left quietly.

"Do you want to go baby?" whispered Chris to Cimber.

"No baby let's do this!" Cimber said with confidence.

"I'm atheist… this is bull shit!" yelled one of the kids as he left.

The General watched them leave then went on with his speech.

"Now… we will review the Demons that we have documents of

so you know what you're up against. When you know what you're up against you will be sent out. You have three days to learn. We will test you all and determine what you will be. Some of you will be researchers who tell us more about these Demons or Demons we have not yet documented. And some will be scouts who protect the researchers. And the others will be Exterminators. Your job will be to eradicate every damn Demon you see, along with hostiles. Only the true bad ass's in this room will be exterminators. You will all be given a group to stick with. Those of you who pay attention and pass the final exam in three days will be sent to the island and those who fail will be sent home. The first test begins today. Today does not count as one of the three days. If the girls will please exit the room and report to room 35 you will be given your test and classes separately. After class report to the cafeteria to find your room." said General Patten.

"Bye baby," said Cimber to Chris as she left.

All the girls left the room.

"Now boys if you would please come up and grab a pencil and paper," said General Patten.

Chris walked up with everyone else and grabbed a test packet.

"The test has math science and Literature in it. It has five hundred questions so good luck!" said General Patten.

Chris sat down and began to take the test.

In the girls room the same thing was happening.

Five hours later Chris finished the test. He was the tenth one out of twenty three of the boys to finish. He handed his paper to the General. And walked out then headed to the cafeteria. Once he arrived he started looking at the room number sheet.

"How was the test?" a voice from behind him said.

"It was a little difficult he," said as he turned around.

When he did he saw the girl standing there that was staring at him earlier.

"Hi I'm CJ," she said.

"Hey I'm Chris," he said as he smiled at her.

"Well I'm going to check my room number and head to it," She said.

"Ok," said Chris. "I hope to see you again soon," he said to her.

"He-he me too," she said as she giggled smiling at him.

Chris walked out and headed down to his room. He had room 146... He got to his room and opened the door then walked in, and in their another kid sat on the top bunk.

"I call top bunk!" the kid yelled. "I'm Travis by the way,"

Chris looked at him.

"Hi I'm Chris," Chris replied.

"Guess we are stuck in the close we came in, because the closet is empty and they gave us no close," said Travis.

"Well I'm in my favorite clothes anyways," said Chris.

He was wearing his tight cut off shorts that went a little past his knees. And his black leather fingerless studded gloves along with his black studded wristband, and black spiked ankle bracelets. He had black skateboarding brand shoes with red and black checkered laces and he wore a black hat that said bullet in red letters that he wore slightly to the left, and had both ears pierced and had his black and red checkered belt along with his black short sleeve button up shirt. He also wore a silver cross necklace and a silver ring on his right ring finger.

He got in his bed and pulled out his phone and texted Cimber.

"Baby you done?" said the text to Cimber.

"Yea just finished," she said.

"How did you do?" Chris text back.

"Meh I don't know," she replied.

"But baby I'm tired I'm going to head to bed," she text.

"Okay baby I love you!" he text.

"I love you to!" she text back.

They both went to bed to prepare for tomorrow. The next three days they had hard work to do.

Chapter 4 — Training Day 1

"GET UP!" Banging sounds came from the door and you can hear General Patten's voice yelling to get up.

"Holly hell..." said Chris.

"What the shit!" said Travis as he accidently rolled over the side of the bunk bed and fell on the concrete floor.

Chris got up and walked over as he was half asleep. He threw on his shirt and already had his pants on since he slept in them.

"Travis, dude why are you naked...?" Chris asked.

"Because this is how I always sleep, I can't sleep in clothes," he said.

"Why not?" asked Chris.

"Because I can't, I find it uncomfortable," said Travis.

"Get up and get outside now!" yelled General Patten.

Both boys walked out the room dressed and ready.

"Fallow me boys to the training field," said General Patten.

Chris and Travis got behind him along with all the other boys. They stopped by two more rooms and the General retrieved four more boys. They followed General Patten out a pair of double doors outside to an obstacle course.

"I want you boys to complete this course as fast as you can. I will send you all individually so I can clock all of you... Dillon! You're first!" yelled General Patten at one of the boys.

Boy after boy went through the course then it came Chris's turn.

"Chris you're up!" yelled the General.

He began to go through the obstacle course, all the other boys watched, amazed by how fast he was climbing the walls and crawling under the barbwire and running through the tires and swinging on the rope. There were so many obstacles... Chris's finally finished and came around.

"Good God son!" exclaimed the General. "That was the fastest damn time I have ever seen someone do this course."

"Thank you sir," replied Chris.

The General finished up with the rest of the boys.

Later on at the girl's course, Cimber was up for the same course on the other side of the Military base.

"Ok Cimber!" yelled Lieutenant Clair.

Cimber ran through the course, she struggled on some parts but still did a decent job. She finished the course and Lieutenant Clair clocked her.

"Decent Cimber but not impressive," said the Lieutenant.

"Yes mam..." said Cimber.

"CJ your up!" yelled the Lieutenant.

CJ ran through the course and did an amazing job. When she finished the Lieutenant clocked her.

"Impressive CJ but nothing special... That's an average time. But still the best I've seen out of the rest of these girls," said the Lieutenant.

CJ walked back to the back of the group with the other girls that finished while the Lieutenant finished up.

"Nice time..." said Cimber.

"Thanks," replied CJ breathing heavily.

"I'm Cimber," she said to CJ.

"I'm CJ," CJ replied.

"Alright girls, let's head to the Cafeteria for lunch," said the

Lieutenant.

Back with the General, he had the boys in the meeting room.

"Alright Chris that was the best time I have seen in my life. You have amazing athletic abilities," said the General. "Now you can all return to your rooms and prepare for tomorrow... No lunch till after 1:00 P.M the girls are still eating.'

"Sir?" said one of the kids raising his hands.

"Yes Chad?" answered General Patten.

"Why are we separated from the girls?" asked Chad.

"Because chad... boys and girls distract each other, we want to keep the boys and the girls separate so there are no distractions, so everyone is working at their hardest," he answered to Chad.

"Yes sir," Chad replied.

"Ok off to lunch boys its 1:00," announced the General.

The boys went to lunch and afterwards returned to their rooms.

"Forget this…" said Travis crawling into his bunk bed.

"What's up Travis?" Chris asked.

"I hate this shit. I will die…." Travis replied.

"Why so negative dude?" said Chris.

"Eh I don't know bro… I just get negative sometimes," replied Travis.

"Well I'm going to sleep on it dude."

"All right," said Chris.

He picked up his cell phone and texted Cimber.

"Night baby, I love you." he text.

"Night baby, Love you too!" she replied.

They both went to bed to prepare for the next day.

Chapter 5 — Training Day 2.

Bang, bang, bang the boys woke up again to the sound of the door banging. Travis once again rolled off the side of the bunk bed naked.

"CRAP!" he yelled.

"GET UP!" yelled the General.

"Dude do you want to sleep on the bottom bunk...?" asked Chris.

"No dude... I'm good," said Travis.

The boys got dressed and went outside and fallowed the General with everyone else again. This time they went back into the projection room.

"All right boys come up to the front and grab a spiral notebook and a pen," General Patten announced.

All the boys walked up and grabbed one, found a seat and sat down.

"Sit close to the front please," said the General.

The boys in the back moved to the front.

"Alright boys, today's class involves Demon study. Pay attention and take notes because tomorrow you will be given the final exam and this will be on it… You will be learning about the Demons we know about so far… For those of you who become Researchers, will find out about the undiscovered demons and tell us about them," said the General as he garbed the slideshow clicker and the projection screen turned on.

"Ok now," he said as he started his lecture. "There are forty five Demons that we know about so far. The first one…"

He clicked the remote and the first Demon slid on the screen.

"This is a Hell Hound," said the General.

It looked like a Rottweiler dog but it had red fur and pure red eyes, with a black stomach, and long tail.

"These are some meanest sons of bitches," the General went on. "They will tear you limb from limb in a matter of seconds... Now one thing to remember about any Demon, Is that they can cut or bite through anything. Rock seems to be their hardest object to get through... They will chew through an armored tank in five minutes, depending on a Demon."

He clicked the remote.

"This is a black Dragon... Now he can bite a tank in half. Be very careful of dragons, they breath fire, and have scales stronger then steel," the General went on.

They reviewed Demons for sixteen hours.

After sixteen hours. The General finished up the final demon.

"Alright boys, you have five hours left of day light. I suggest you use the time to study... Tomorrow at 11:00 a.m., you will report to this room and take your final exam. It has five hundred questions. After you're done you will return to the cafeteria and sit on the boy's side, and wait to hear what you will become. I will not wake you up this time in the morning," the General said. "You will report here at 11:00 a.m. responsibly or you will fail. Now go study," said the general.

The boys returned to their room and studied their material for the rest of the day.

"Dude let's do this!" said Travis with excitement.

"Well you've changed your mind aside from yesterday I see," said Chris.

"Hell yea dude," said Travis. "But it's like 11:30 p.m. bro, I'm hitting the bunk," he said.

"Same here dude," said Chris as he put down his spiral notebook that he has been studying.

He text Cimber goodnight and went to bed.

Chapter 6 — Training Day 3. The Final Exam

"Travis! Travis!" Chris yelled.

"What!?!" Travis yelled as he woke up.

"Dude get up its 10:38 a.m. dude!" Chris Exclaimed.

"Fuck!" yelled Travis as he jumped out of bed.

The boys quickly showered and got dressed and reported to the study room.

"Ok their they are," said the General. "Come up front and get your exams," he said to them.

Chris grabbed his exam, found a seat and got started. He made his way past the first question.

Several minutes later at 11:08 a.m., two boys came in the room.

"Troy and Jonathan... your late," said the General. "Report to room 12 to get a helicopter ride back home."

"But sir please its only 11:08," said Troy.

"I said 11:00 a.m. Not 11:08..." the General replied.

"But sir..." said Jonathan.

"DO NOT ARGUE WITH ME!" yelled the General. "Room 12, now! You're going home." the General said.

The boys left the room and everyone else resumed their test.

Seven hours later Chris had finished the test. He walked up to the general who was sitting on the edge of the stage, and took Chris's paper as he handed it to him.

"Thanks Chris. Now you may head to the cafeteria," said General Patten.

Chris made his way into the cafeteria and sat down at one of the lunch tables. He along with three other boys had finished. Most of the girls have already finished as well. Only two girls where left and Cimber was one of them still in.

An hour later mostly all the boys where finished now and Cimber walked in. She waved at Chris and smiled and he waved back. He looked passed her and saw CJ looking at him. He smiled at her and waved… she waved and smiled back. Behind Cimber were the last three boys and behind them was the General. He walked up to the front of the cafeteria with the score sheets.

"All right now…" said the General. "Some of you will make it and some of you will be headed home," he went on.

He called out the first name.

"Jessica," announced the General. "You passed with an eighty-six percent on the final exam but your athletic training passed with a fifty-four percent, you will be a Researcher and will be in group one. Please report to room 111 for your Researcher training for the rest of the day."

She walked out and left…

The General went on for two hours, and then he came to CJ's name.

"CJ," General Patten announced. "You passed your exam with a ninety-eight percent, very well done! And you passed your athletics with an eighty-nine percent. However, you did so well on the final, we half to put you as a Researcher. You will be in group 4. We need your knowledge... Please report to room 111."

She walked out and reported to her room.

After two more people, Cimber was called.

"Cimber," said the General. "You passed your final with an eighty percent and made a seventy-six percent on your athletics. You will be a Scout and be put in group four. Please report to room 115."

She smiled as she got up and left the room, excited that she did not fail at least.

After she left the General had finally called out Chris's name.

"Chris," the General said. "You made a ninety percent on your final, but made a one-hundred percent on your athletics. That's amazing soldier! I am going to put you in Extermination."

Chris smiled widely.

"Please stay in the cafeteria, you will be with me," said the General.

The General finished up the rest of the boys and girls, and only the Exterminators remained in the cafeteria.

"I have nine Exterminators it seems... three girls and six boys," said General Patten. "You do not need any further training; now since you are Exterminators you will not need any groups... you will go it alone because you are strong enough to do it independently. You may report to your rooms and have the rest of the day to yourself... Report to the Air hanger tomorrow, all of you."

They all went back to their rooms. When Chris got their Travis was laying on the bunk bed.

"What did you get dude?" Travis asked Chris.

"I'm an Exterminator dude!" Chris exclaimed.

"Wow bro," said Travis. "I got scout... How many went home?" Travis asked.

"Only one," said Chris.

"Who was it?" asked Travis.

"It was Derek," Chris replied.

"What did he make?" Travis asked.

"He made a thirty-four percent on his final exam and sixty-five percent on his athletics," said Chris.

Travis and Chris laughed.

"Wow what a fail," said Travis.

"I know right? How did he get recruited?" replied Chris.

"I have no idea but dude, I'm headed to bed," said Travis.

"Night man," Chris replied.

"Night dude," said Travis.

Chris grabbed his cell phone and saw that Cimber had already text him. The text read.

"I miss you!"

Chris replied. "I miss you too baby! Congratz on becoming a scout!"

"Thanks babe," she replied. "What did you get?" she asked.

Chris replied. "I got an exterminator."

Cimber replied. "WOW! GRATZ BABY!"

"Thanks," replied Chris. "I'm going to head to bed baby," He text.

"Ok baby, I love you goodnight!" replied Cimber.

"Love you too baby! Goodnight!" he replied.

"My phone is almost dead by the way baby." she text back.

"Ok babe, I'm going to miss you." Chris replied.

"I'll miss you too baby! Good luck tomorrow!" Cimber replied.

"Good night baby," Chris text back.

He rolled over and went to sleep.

Chapter 7 – The Island

Chris and Travis woke up and showered and got dressed. They reported to the Air hanger with everyone else.

"Ok!" said the General. "Scouts follow Lieutenant Clair to get your gear. Researchers follow Corporal Tina. And Exterminators follow Me." the General announced.

Everyone followed who they were supposed to and the Exterminators followed the General into an armory.

"Ok soldiers," said General Patten. "Now gear up. This is the armory take what you can carry and grab a back pack and fill it with what you need."

"Excuse me sir?" asked a boy named Aaron.

"Yes Aaron?" asked the General.

"Do we get Uniforms?" Aaron asked.

"No sir, you will go in what you came in," said the General.

"But it's dirty…" said Aaron.

"Tuff it out," said General Patten.

"Yes sir," said Aaron.

Chris grabbed a shotgun and a 1911 pistol. He slung the shotgun over his back and put the pistol around the back of his waist. He attached a combat knife to his right leg on his calf, right above his spiked ankle bracelet. He grabbed a backpack and put a health kit in it and some MRE's, some ammo and a tinderbox. He clipped a small keychain compass to the side of his left pocket.

All of the soldiers where geared up. He fallowed the General back out to the hanger with the rest of the soldiers, the Scouts and the Researchers stood geared up and waiting. Chris and Cimber waved at each other.

"Ok," General Patten began to announce. "You all are about to be left on an island that is inhabited by Demons. You will not be picked up until the Hell Hole's location has been reported. Anyone who reports falsely will not be picked up. Once the location is reported, an air strike will fly over and destroy the location so get 3 miles out of the area. The Taliban forces will try to claim this island, so destroy all and any hostiles you come across. Be prepared, stay alert, and do not panic or freak out, or this island will destroy you before you can say, "Oh shit," The General announced. "Oh and one more thing," he said. "The island's location is where the sun doesn't hit much, so day will be shorted than normal.... Now!"

He walked over to the first helicopter that started up.

"You will be flown to the island and you will Para shoot down to it. Now in the first helicopter team one load up! Let's GO! GO! GO!" The General exclaimed.

Team one loaded up into the helicopter and it took off. The next helicopter was team two, then next was team three, then team four. Chris watched and waved at Cimber as she loaded up and took off. Then team five, five helicopters took off.

"Now Exterminators follow me!" said General Patten.

The Exterminates loaded up in the helicopter with the

General. They buckled up in their seats and the helicopter took off. The helicopter ride took nine hours. At 8:30 p.m. they reached the island.

"Ok, now everyone grab a Para shoot!" said the General.

All the boys grabbed one and buckled it on.

"Good luck and God be with you boys!" said General Patten.

They all began to jump out, Chris was the last one. He jumped out and opened his Para shoot; he landed on the south west side. He looked up when he landed and watched as the General and the rest of the helicopters went on back to the base in Arizona. The sun was about to go down in twenty minutes. Cimber who was on the other side of the island had formed with her group.

CHapter 8 — The terror of the first night.

The sun had set and the first night had started.

"Oh God..." said Chris.

The sounds around him were spine chilling howls and screams of Demons that echoed around the island. Chris then begins to hear a snarling sound behind him. He turns around and there staring at him is a Hell Hound. Chris swallowed deeply and the Hell Hound ran at him, it jumped on him knocking him down, pinning him to the ground. He pulled out his pistol and shot it in the head and it did not die. It started biting at him and he grabbed its throat and held its head away but it was so strong and getting closer to biting his face off. He shot it three more times in the head and it still lived. He had to kill it, and fast as its mouth was getting closer to his face and snapping down at him. He pulled his combat knife out of his holster on his right leg. He stabbed the hell hound in the head and it still stood there snapping at him.

"It won't die!" yelled Chris.

He then took the knife and slashed at the Hell Hounds neck and cut it almost off. The Hell Hound still stood there. He slashed one more time and cut off its head. The Hell Hounds head stopped snapping and its body fell to the ground and disintegrated into ashes. Chris dropped the head and it fell to the ground and disintegrated as well.

"Good God... you half to cut off the head to kill them..." said Chris to himself.

He then picked up his pistol and put it in his holster. He then heard a screaming sound behind him. He turned around and there staring at him was a big Demon standing behind him. It stood like a human... It then slashed its long claws at Chris. He jumped back and put up his knife as fast as he could because he knows he could not reach that Demons neck with that knife while it was swinging its huge twelve inch claws as him. He pulled out his shotgun, when he did the Demon swung at him. He held up his shotgun and blocked it; he got knocked to the ground. Chris got back up right away and pointed the shotgun at the Demons head and fired. He blew off part of the Demons head but it still stood and kept swinging its huge claws at Chris. Chris dodged them and fired at the Demons head again and blew off the other half of its head. The Demon then dropped to the ground dead without a head on his shoulders. The body then disintegrated... He looked up and saw red piercing eyes in the darkness of the jungle looking at him. Chris then ran, a Demon then began to chase after him; it caught up with him and grabbed him by his back pack. Chris slipped out of his back pack as fast as he could and kept running, leaving his back pack behind. The Demon dropped it and some Demon dogs got ahold of it and started eating the MRE's out of it. He ran into the jungle and looked behind him to see if the Demons where still after him. While he was looking behind him; he ran into something in front of him. He fell to the ground and looked up. All of a sudden this big black figure moved in the darkness. It opened up its mouth and a fiery red light came out of it. Chris started to run when fire came out of its mouth and hit him. It got the back of his shirt and burned a hole in it. Chris dropped to the ground, rolled out the fire and got back up right away. He kept running and while he was he could hear the sounds of gun shots and screaming going on as the Demons where killing some of the others that where on the island. Chris kept running when he came across an abandon military base like structure. It had only two walls on two sides, it looked more like a tent made out of metal with a bunch of junk in it. He ran towards it and found a bomb shelter in the middle of it that went down into the ground. It was sealed with a metal door. He opened it real fast before the Demons could see him and went inside. He shut it and locked it from the inside. He could hear the Demons outside screeching and screaming. He worried about Cimber and hoped that she was still alive.

He looked down the hallway of the bomb shelter and saw a desk at the end with a skeleton sitting at it. He walked up to it and found a recorder sitting on the desk with some paper's and a pencil. He pushed play on the recorder and a voice came on and it said.

"This island is dammed…. There is no way to kill the Demons with guns…. You can't kill them with fire either…. You need to have a weapon that has a blade…. A big one that you can reach them with… They have good reach and could kill you before you could take a knife to them…"

The recording ended… Chris grabbed the skeleton and threw it out of the chair. He sat down at the Desk and began to draw plans for some weapons he could use.

"Shot guns are the one gun that seems to work…" Chris said to himself as he began to draw.

Meanwhile Cimber was fighting Demons, she got her group and they ran into a cave.

"COME ON CJ AND ERICA!" yelled Cimber. "Come on guys!" She continued to yell.

CJ, Cimber, Travis, Dillon, and Jacob all got in the cave. While their other member Erica was making her way into the cave a Demon quickly grabbed her by the foot and pulled her to the ground.

"HELP ME!" Erica yelled with a voice full of fear.

Cimber grabbed her hand but before she could get a good grip, a Demon quickly drug her off into the darkness of the jungle.

"NO! ERICA!" Cimber yelled as she fired her guns at the Demons, hitting some of them. They all watched and listened as the sounds of Erica's screams could be heard in the distance. Demons began to surround the entrance of the cave.

"We are trapped in here!" yelled Jacob.

"Oh no we are not!" Travis said as he quickly devised a plan to keep the Demons from getting them. Travis fired a grenade from his grenade launcher at the bottom of his P90, at the roof of the cave and blew it down, caving them into the cave. They all sat down and panted from running and fighting off the Demons.

"There is no way to kill them..." said Cimber.

"I killed one with a shot gun..." said Travis.

"We need to rest and figure this out tomorrow morning when we can get out," said CJ.

"I'll start a fire," said Jacob as he pulled some supplies out of his backpack.

Jacob started the fire and they gathered around it and all got ready to sleep.

"I'll stay up and watch," said Dillon.

"Alright," replied Cimber.

Chapter 9 – New weapons.

The next morning Chris woke up and crawled out of the bomb shelter with his plans for some new weapons. He began to look around the abandon base and saw a cutting torch and a welder. He crawled back down the bomb shelter and grabbed the combat knife off the skeletal remains of the soldier. He came back out and grabbed the torch and the welder. He then took the knife from the soldier remains and broke the blade from the handle. He looked around and saw a roll of chain; He cut six foot of chain off of it. He then welded the knife blade to one end of the chain and the knife handle to the other.

He now had made a whip like weapon. Now he can reach the Demons within six foot of him. He then took the blow torch and cut out a sword blade from the wall of the base. It was made out of steel so it would be prefect for a sword. The blade was about two feet and five inches long. He had no handle for it though. He looked around and found a rusty knife lying under one of the tables. He broke off the rusty blade and welded the handle of the knife to the sword blade he had just cut from the wall. The sword was strong but dull; he then found a grinder.

From the looks of the tools around him he could tell that the base was still being built.

He took the grinder and grinded down the sides of the sword blade and created the edges, he made them very sharp and perfect. It almost felt complete... He took some tin from the roof and shaped it around the blade making a sword case. He decided it needed a more professional look. He took off his shirt to use to cover the outside of the case since he had a hole in the back of it from wear the fire burnt. He decided to go shirtless... He took the extra strap off his shotgun and latched it through the sword case and put it on his back. He faced the sword upside down so he could grab it easier, but the sword did not stay in the case... So he took some magnets that was used to pick up scrap metal bits; and welded them to the outside edge of the sword case to hold in the sword. He attacked another big piece of metal to the side of the sword case in about the middle so he could wear the whip wrapped around his chest like the strap of the sword case, and the magnets could hold the blade of the whip. He attached one more magnet to the front of the strap on his chest so the whip handle could be held.

He almost felt that he had everything he needed. Then he looked at his shotgun.

"Hmm it would be use full if I attached a blade under the shot gun so I could hit Demons with it since the shotgun takes two hands..." Chris said to himself.

He cut out another blade from the wall, about the length of the shotgun barrel; and grinded it down to a sharp edge. He then welded it together with some little bars to put some distance between it and the bottom of the shotgun so he could still pump the shotgun.

"Perfect!" said Chris.

He left the weapons on the table to cool off since they were still hot from just being made. Luckily the base was built right on the shore of the island. He walked over to the ocean with a bucket and got some water, then brought it back to the base and cooled off his new weapons. He had just got them on when all of a sudden he heard a noise... He looked out above the ocean and saw a helicopter coming in the distance.

"Oh no..." Chris said to himself.

The helicopter approached the shore and began to land by the base. While it was coming down the Taliban soldiers inside of it began to shoot at him with machine guns. He ran and jumped behind a table and then crawled behind the wall of the building.

"Guess now I can test out my new weapons," Chris said to himself.

He ran up the wall and grabbed hold of the top edge of the roof. He crawled up and stood on top of the roof. He grabbed his pistol and his whip... The Taliban soldiers got out of the helicopter...

There was six of them... plus the two in the front of the helicopter, the pilot and the co-pilot.

Chris ran and jumped off the side of the roof and swung his whip. He landed on the ground and his whip came down on one of the soldiers, cutting him in half. The soldiers began to shoot at him. He managed to keep out of the way of the bullets. He then turned around and swung the whip with him and cut off the soldier's head that was behind him. He took his pistol and shot the other Taliban by the front of the helicopter in the head, right in between his eyes... Chris then jumped through the center of the helicopter where it was open from where the soldiers got out. He jumped through to the other side of the helicopter and shot the first Taliban he saw in the head, same place as the last one. He shot the other one behind that last one next. Then he swung his whip at the last Taliban and cut off his head.

He walked over to the front side of the helicopter and shot the Co-Pilot in the side of the head, the bullet went through the co-pilot then right into the pilots head, killing them both with one bullet.

"I think I like these new weapons," Chris said to himself.

He searched the bodies for ammo and anything else. on one of them he came across, had black lipstick in his pocket.

"Why the hell is he carrying this?" Chris asked to himself. "Oh well I can find a good use for it."

He put it in his pocket, then he heard another noise that sounded like something traveling really fast through the air. He looked up at the sky beyond the ocean and saw another helicopter. But this one had missiles on it... and one of them had just been fired and headed towards him.

"SHIT!" yelled Chris.

He ran and jumped over a table and flipped it over in front of him to use as cover. The missile then hit the landed helicopter and blew it up. The fire raged around Chris as he lay behind the table.

The fire then cleared, he got up and looked at one of the body's that he killed and noticed that the fire took off the whole front half of its body from the explosion, and all you can see where its exposed skeletal remains on the front half.

"Damn..." said Chris to himself.

The helicopter that shot the missile flew over the island. Chris then walked up to a broken piece of glass lying on the ground from the helicopter, and took out the black lipstick. He looked at his reflection and drew gothic arrows around his eyes that pointed down his cheeks. He then colored it in and put away the lipstick back in his pocket.

"War paint!" said Chris to himself.

He then began his journey through the jungle.

Meanwhile Cimber and the others had just woken up and where trying to get out of the cave.

"How are we going to get out?" Dillon asked.

"You guys this is simple," said CJ.

She reached over and grabbed one of Travis's grenades.

"Watch..." said CJ.

She pulled the pin and threw it at the rubble.

"OH MY GOD, WHAT THE HECK ARE YOU DOING?" yelled

Cimber.

"SHE THREW A LIVE GRANADE!" yelled Jacob.

"TAKE COVER!" Travis yelled.

They all jumped behind the nearest rock. The grenade exploded and blew away some of the rubble. Now light was peering through the rubble.

"Ok… I think we can dig away the rest," said Cimber.

CJ grabbed another grenade and pulled the pin and threw it at the remaining rubble.

"OH MY GOD!" yelled Cimber.

They all ducked behind a rock again. The grenade went off and the rubble cleared away this time.

"It's gone!" CJ announced with joy as she smiled.

"Your grenade happy!" yelled Travis.

"I did it!" said CJ with joy.

Travis glared at her.

"Ok guys…" said Cimber. "We need to start a fire and find a way to put a door on this cave so we can stay safe at night."

"We can rig a pulley system." said Travis.

"Yea," said Dillon. "We can pulley a rock down in front of the door."

"Perfect!" said Cimber.

They looked around the side of the mountain for a rock they could use.

"That one!" said CJ pointing to a big boulder.

"Ok that one…" said Cimber.

"I have some good rope in my bag." said Jacob.

"Ok, we can pull down this palm tree and use it," said Dillon.

"Perfect! But I need food!" said Jacob.

"Ok, if you boys get to work on it I'll go find some food," said Cimber.

"Done deal," said Travis.

Cimber walked out into the jungle in search of food and CJ started a fire for when Cimber got back so they could cook.

Meanwhile Chris was walking through the forest and smelt the fire.

"People…" Chris said to himself as he began to fallow the smell.

He fallowed the smell and after several minutes he came to the fire, and saw CJ sitting there. She looked up at him and smiled really widely at him.

"It's you," said Chris.

"Hi!" said CJ with excitement.

"It's good to see you alive," Chris said.

"It's good to see you too cutie!" said CJ.

Chris blushed a little.

"Do you need a place to stay?" CJ asked him.

"Sure I will hang with you," Chris replied. "I don't think anyone else is left alive…"

"Yea… I think we are the last ones left…" said CJ.

"I need to find my bag though," said Chris.

"Your bag?" asked CJ.

"Yea my back pack, it has my phone in it," Chris replied.

"Oh! You have a phone?" CJ asked.

"Yea," said Chris.

"Can you put your number in my phone?" asked CJ as she pulled her phone out.

"Sure," said Chris smiling.

He grabbed her phone and put his number in it.

"Yay!" said CJ as she took her phone back from him.

"I need to find my way back to my back pack," Chris said to her.

"Well Jacob can help!" CJ said.

"Jacob?" Chris asked.

"JACOB, COME HERE!" yelled CJ.

Jacob came down from the mountain side where he was trying to help Dillon and Travis roll down the rock to use as a door.

"Wow there is people up there," Chris said.

"Jacob has a map of the island," Said CJ.

"Ok," said Chris.

Jacob came down and approached CJ and Chris.

"What's up?" Jacob asked.

"Hey dude," Chris replied.

"He needs to see the map!" said CJ to Jacob.

"What for?" Jacob asked.

"I need to find my bag dude," said Chris.

"Ok, no problem," Jacob replied as he pulled a map out of his bag.

Jacob unrolled the map and laid it out on the ground.

"Where did you lose it?" Jacob asked.

"Well I landed somewhere around here," said Chris as he pointed at the map. "And then I ran over this direction."

"Ok dude, that's directly west from hear." said Jacob.

"Ok, thanks bro," Chris replied.

"No problem dude," said Jacob.

"Well I am going to go get my bag and I'll be back," said Chris.

"Ok, be careful," said CJ.

She hugged him and he hugged her back and went off into the jungle.

"You better hurry before night hits!" said Jacob as he watched Chris walk off.

"Ok!" replied Chris as he disappeared into the jungle.

About twenty minutes after he had left, Cimber came back to the camp site with some fruit.

"Aw! No meet?" asked CJ.

"No," said Cimber. "The Demons killed all the animals that where inhabitants of this island."

"Oh..." replied CJ.

"Well at least there is fruit..." said Travis.

They finished the door rig and came down and enjoyed the fruit that Cimber had brought back.

Chapter 10 – The Back Pack

Chris traveled across the island for three hours before he finally came to the location where he landed. He saw his Para shoot mangled in the tree then he began to trace his steps from when he got attacked. He looked around and finally came to his bag. He sifted through it and pulled out ammo and then found some deodorant and put it on. He sifted through the bag some more and came across his phone, and put it in his pocket. After getting his phone he took out the duct tape and taped the shot gun magazine's together on opposite ends so he could carry more, he loaded up all he could into the shot gun magazine and got his radio (to call an air strike) out of the bag, then went on his way, leaving his bag there.

Meanwhile group four was working on getting their cave ready for the night.

"Guys the sun is about to set," said Cimber.

"But Chris isn't back yet," said CJ.

"CHRIS?!" said Cimber with hope. "I'm so glad he's alive..."

"You know Chris?" CJ asked.

"DUDE CHRIS IS ALIVE?" asked Travis.

"You know him too Travis?" asked CJ.

"He's my boyfriend..." said Cimber.

"He was my roommate," said Travis.

"Where was he? How did you find him? Where did he go?" Cimber began to ask.

"Um he found us by the smell of the fire; he just set off to find his bag so he could get his stuff out of it." CJ answered her.

"Well it's almost dark now and we are going to half to leave him out," said Jacob.

"He's right..." said Travis.

"Yea he made it through the first night just fine and I know him well, he's a good fighter too," said Cimber as she began to tear up.

"NO… we can't do that!" yelled CJ.

"We are going to half to… we half to survive, and if he comes he can yell at us from behind the door and we will open it," said Dillon.

"Ok…" said CJ with a hint of sadness in her voice.

Cimber gave her a strange look.

"Ok well we half to get in the cave now…" said Cimber.

They all went in and shut the cave then started a fire. CJ grabbed her phone and text Chris.

"Hey did you find your bag yet? Are you on your way?" she text.

Chris felt his phone vibrate, he grabbed it and read the text.

"Yea I found it and I am about an hour away," He text back to her.

"It will be dark in like five minutes…" she text back.

"Don't worry about me, I can take care of myself Hun," he text back.

"Ok please hurry... I'm worried about you," she text.

The sun went down and howling and screaming noises began to echo throughout the island once again. Chris kept walking when a Demon came out of the shadows of the jungle. Chris glared into the piercing red eyes of the Demon. Then another one came out of the darkness from behind him. More and more Demons began to come out of the darkness of the jungle. Chris looked around him and saw that he was surrounded by fifteen or more Demons.

"Bring it on... I've got new weapons to try out," Chris said.

He pulled out his sword and slung out his whip. A Demon ran at him and lunged at him jumping in the air. He swung his sword and cut the first Demons head off. Then more and more began to come at him. He had seven coming at him at once. He dodged one Demons lashing arms and cut its head off with the whip. Then he swung the whip behind him and cut off two Demons heads at once, that where standing beside each other. Then a Hell Hound jumped at him from behind he quickly turned around and struck it in the neck cutting of its head. The Demons body's dropped and disintegrated as he killed them. He continued to fight when a Demon came flying out of the air and began to swoop down at him. Chris threw his whip over his shoulder and wrapped it around his chest. A Demon behind his struck him in the back and knocked him down. He got up and stuck the Demon, cutting its head off. As soon as he killed it, the Demon flying down at him in the air, came swooping back down and grabbed him around the arms and took him to the air. The Demon took Chris to the other side of the island. Chris struggled and tried to hit the Demon with his sword. He continued to swing at the Demon when a fiery red light caught his eye. He looked and saw for a quick glimpse a light peering through the trees. The Demon then dropped Chris. Chris then began to plummet down to the ground and tried to quickly think of a way to save himself. He quickly devised a plan to take his whip and wrap it around a tree branch, swinging himself to the ground. He took out his whip and then quickly approached the top of the jungle. He threw his whip at the nearest tree and wrapped it around a branched and slid down to the ground perfectly as planned. He stumbled a bit when he landed and fell to the ground but quickly got back up and looked around him, then saw that once again he was surrounded by Demons. He pulled out his shotgun and got ready to fight.

The first Demon came at him and he swung his shot gun and hit the Demon with the blade welded to the bottom of the shotgun. The next Demon came at him and he jumped up in the air and kicked it to the ground. It got back up and lunged at him; he pumped the shot gun and blew the Demons head off. He continued to fight Demons for an hour. He glimpsed up real quick and saw a helicopter in the distance beyond the horizon. The Taliban's where coming... but he knew that they are nothing compared to the Demons gnashing and swinging at him. The fight between him and the Demons went on when he looked up at the horizon and saw the sun light peering over it. The sun was about to come up and the fight between him and the Demons that he had been struggling and fighting with to stay alive was about to be over...

Chapter 11 – Hostages.

The sun began to come up and Chris watched as the Demons ran back to the Hell Hole. He paid attention to what directions the Demons where heading. He looked at his compass and saw that they were headed west. He looked to the sky and saw the Demons that could fly diving down into the jungle. He then knew where the Hell Hole was, but still needed to find it to confirm the exact location, so when he call's in the air strike he doesn't blow up the whole north side of the island.

The sun then rose and all the Demons that had not yet made it back to the Hell Hole disintegrated as the sunlight hit them. He looked at his compass for the direction of east; he then began to head that way when he saw more helicopters coming and watched them as the landed on the north east side of the island. Just then a vehicle came out of the jungle with a mounted machine gun on it and began to shoot at Chris. Chris ran and ducked behind a rock. He took out his pistol and cocked back the top of it. He poked up from behind the rock and took two quick shots. He shot the guy on the turret in the head; then shot the driver in the head through the windshield. The vehicle drove out of control, flipped and rolled over on its right side. Five Taliban soldiers crawled out of the crashed vehicle, two of them were very injured and three of them lay dead in the vehicle; two from being shot and one from the impact of the crash.

Chris walked out from behind the rock. He began to walk towards the crashed vehicle. The three that were in good condition began to rise up their weapons to shoot him. Chris took three quick shots and shot all three of them. He walked over to the vehicle and saw one soldier lying against it bleeding really badly. The soldier looked up at him and pointed a pistol at him while his hand shook from loss of blood. Chris grabbed the gun and pulled it easily out of his hand. He took the soldiers pistol from him and pointed it at his head. He looked into the soldiers eyes and pulled the trigger, killing the soldier... He dropped the soldier's pistol on his lap and walked around to the other side of the truck. The last soldier was lying on the ground with the lower half of his body still in the vehicle window with glass sticking into his body from the broken window. Chris took out his pistol to shoot the soldier. But before he could pull the trigger the soldier began to cough up blood and died.

Chris searched all the body's and found shoot gun ammo and pistol ammo. He loaded up his guns to capacity and made his way east, back to the camp site.

Back at the campsite, group four had just come out of the cave. As soon as they got out some Taliban soldiers who had saw the smoke from the camp fire that burned all night, had their guns pointed at the group.

"CJ you didn't put out the campfire..." said Cimber.

"Crap we are outnumbered... we got to surrender..." said Travis.

"Sorry..." said CJ.

The group put their hands up and the Taliban's took their weapons and took them as hostages. The Taliban's set up a camp near the cave so they could use it for when the Demons came. For four hours they set up the camp. Stocking up their weapons and putting up their tents. Group four sat near the smaller tent tied up in chairs outside.

"Shit we lost the island..." said Dillon.

"No... Chris is still out there..." said CJ.

"You haven't heard from him for hours last night after the sun went down," said Travis.

"What...?" said Cimber with anger, "your texting my boyfriend?"

"I was trying to make sure he's alright," said CJ.

"Yea he's fine..." said Cimber.

"Yea I believe he will save us," said CJ.

"I'm sure you do..." replied Cimber.

"What's that supposed to mean...?" asked CJ.

"Guys stop fighting..." said Dillon.

Meanwhile Chris traveled across the island for five hours when he finally came up to the camp site. Before he had crawl through the bushes he heard the voices of the Taliban soldiers. He snuck up through the bushes and saw the camp site and saw the group tied up by the tents. He stood up from behind the bushes and walked out of them towards the group. One of the soldiers that saw him began to yell and pointed his gun at him. The group looked up and saw Chris standing there.

"CHRIS!" yelled CJ and Cimber at the same time.

"RUN!" yelled CJ.

Chris stood their staring down the soldiers as they pointed their guns at him and yelled. He pulled out his whip and his pistol.

"Let's do this..." Chris said.

He swung his whip at the first soldier's gun, the whip wrapped around the barrel of the gun and Chris jerked it out of the Taliban's hand, Chris then shot him in the head with his pistol. The other soldiers began to fire at Chris. Chris took his pistol and shot two of them in the head and jumped into the bushes... The soldiers lost track of him, as he snuck around quietly in the bushes. Chris got as close as he could without being seen or heard, to the biggest group of soldiers. He took out his shot gun and jumped out of the bushes at the group of soldiers and fired his shotgun at the first one blowing a hole in his chest. He lunged at the next soldier and swung the blade on his shot gun at the Taliban's throat, slitting it open. Chris pulled out his pistol after he quickly put up his shotgun, and shot at the next soldier and killed him. He slung back out his whip and lashed the next Taliban's face in half. He threw his whip around and the blade stab straight into another Taliban's chest. He jerked the whip out of the soldier's chest and slung it around him, cutting the next soldiers throat with it. Chris came to another soldier standing there scared readying his gun at Chris. Chris took out his pistol and shot the soldier in the head. He then ran over to the group all tied up on the chairs, he slashed the whip and cut off their ties.

Ten soldiers remained their looking at him getting ready to fire. He took his pistol and shot five times. He managed to shoot four of them, but missed the fifth one. As Chris was readying his pistol to shoot the fifth one, a vehicle drove by with the five remaining soldiers in it. The fifth one hopped in the vehicle, and the vehicle drove off.

"I'm going after them!" yelled Chris.

"Good luck!" yelled Cimber.

"Be careful!" yelled CJ.

Before Chris ran off he saw a RPG launcher with two rockets lying in an ammunition box beside it. One rocket was already loaded into the RPG. Chris grabbed it and the two rockets and ran after the vehicle.

He followed lost track of it but followed the tire tracks to the north east shore of the island, and when get got there he saw four boats loaded up on the shore and unloading Taliban soldier's onto the beach. Chris readied the RPG and fired it; the rocket blew up one boat. The explosion caused the boat next to it to blow up as well. Two boats have been destroyed now. He loaded another rocket into the RPG and blew up the next boat that had just arrived and not yet unloaded soldiers. He loaded up the last rocket, but as he got ready to blow up the last boat, the helicopter with the missiles on it that had tried to blow him up from the first day, was approaching from beyond the ocean.

"Perfect...." Chris said to himself.

Chris readied his RPG and fired it in the air at the helicopter. The rocket flew and hit the helicopter and the helicopter blew up. The debris of the helicopter fell into the ocean. Just then the last boat unloaded a Taliban tank and some armored vehicles with mounted machine guns.

"Holy..." Chris said to himself.

Chris dropped the RPG and ran back to the camp site. Back at the camp site the group was arming their selves back up. Just as they finished Chris came running up.

"RUN! OH MY GOD! RUN!" Chris yelled.

"WHAT, WHAT?!" asked Cimber.

"THEY HAVE TANKS!" Chris replied.

"OH HELL!" Travis yelled.

They all grabbed their stuff quickly and ran.

"I know where the Hell Hole is!" said Chris as they ran.

"Oh my god you found it?" asked CJ.

"Yes, yes!" replied Chris.

"Guys get in that mounted machine gun truck!" yelled Dillon.

"I got the wheel!" said Travis.

"Ok I got the machine gun!" said Dillon.

They all quickly got loaded up into the armored machine gun mounted truck and took off.

"The sun is setting!" yelled CJ.

"Let it set!" yelled Chris. "The Demons can take out the Taliban's."

Chapter 12 – It's Hard to Say Goodbye...

The sun then set and the howling and screaming started again.

"Demons!" yelled Jacob.

The Demons began to come out of the jungle.

"Keep driving, and head west!" yelled Chris.

"Sure thing!" Travis replied.

They headed west and Dillon stayed on the turret shooting the Demons on the turret, not killing them but slowing them down, while Travis ran them over. Jacob started to shoot at the Demons with his AK-47.

"Don't waste your ammo Jacob," said Chris. "You half to

completely decapitate them to kill them."

"Damn…" said Jacob.

They kept driving and a blue Dragon came out of the darkness of the jungle.

"Holy shit!" yelled Travis.

"Fuck!" yelled Cimber.

"Oh my god!" yelled Dillon on the mounted machine gun and began to shoot at it.   The Demon Dragon swung its tail at the truck, hit it and flipped the truck. The truck rolled over, landed upside down, and Dillon who was on the mounted machine gun had his head crushed between the ground and the car. Everyone but Dillon, who was now dead, all crawled out of the wrecked truck. Jacob had his leg pined in-between the ground and the truck.

"Dillon! Jacob!" yelled Travis.

"We half to save Jacob!" yelled CJ.

Chris ran over to the other side of the vehicle to help Jacob out, when all of a sudden a Hell Hound ran up and bit Jacob's neck and ripped his throat out.

"No!" yelled Travis.

Chris swung his whip and cut off the Hell Hounds head. Demons began to surround them but didn't come to close because the dragon had already marked them as its kill by roaring loudly at the other Demons.

The Demons circled around them waiting.

"What's happening?" asked Cimber.

"We are about to be Bar-B-Q...." said Travis.

The dragon opened his mouth and fire began to forum in the back of its throat as it huffed back and got ready to exhale fire onto them. Chris quickly grabbed a grenade off of Travis's belt.

"RUN WEST!" yelled Chris as he pulled the pin of the grenade and arched his arm back to throw it.

Cimber looked into the jungle beyond the wall of Demons and saw an abandon Tank that marked U.S.A on the side.

"Fallow me!" said Cimber as she took off.

Chris threw the grenade into the Dragons mouth and the grenade blew up as soon as it hit the fire in the back of the Dragons throat. The Dragons head blew into pieces and its body fell to the ground and disintegrated.

"Travis give me a grenade!" yelled Cimber.

Travis quickly took a grenade off his belt and tossed it to Cimber and she caught it, pulled the pin then threw it at the wall of Demons blocking them from the tank. The grenade exploded and didn't kill any Demons but it blew them out of the way enough so they could fit through. They made their way through the small path between the Demons before the Demons got to them.

"Get in that tank!" yelled Cimber.

"Fuck yes!" said Travis.

They crawled up onto the tank and got in. Chris manned the big gun and Travis manned the mini mounted machine gun in the back of it. Cimber started up the tank and began to drive it.

"Where did you learn to drive this?" asked CJ.

"Scout training" replied Cimber.

Chris and Travis shot the Demons, keeping them away from the tank.

"I recognize this place!" said Chris.

They drove out into an open field. Chris saw the wrecked vehicle he took out earlier.

"Guys! We are almost their!" yelled Chris.

Just then in front of them, a tank came out of the jungle from behind the wrecked vehicle from earlier, and off in the distance behind it was the tank and armored vehicles that unloaded from the boat at the shore.

"Guys! Taliban's!" yelled Chris.

The Demons began to surround the U.S.A tank, and tear away at it.

"Great we got Demons, now Taliban's to deal with!" yelled Cimber.

"I'd rather deal with Taliban's!" said CJ.

"Same here," replied Chris.

Chris looked off into the distance at the Taliban forces moving towards them. Then noticed how more and more Demons began to surround the Taliban's. Some of the Demons trying to destroy their tank even ran after the Taliban forces.

"They're going for the Taliban's!" said Chris.

"That's good!" said CJ.

"Now we got a distraction to get to the Hell Hole faster, keep heading west!" said Chris.

"Why are they going for the Taliban's now and letting off us anyway?" asked Cimber.

"I don't care, their off us at least." said CJ.

"The Taliban's have more people, more food for the Demons so their more interested in them." said Chris.

Chris watched and noticed that the Demons were beginning to rip apart the Taliban's vehicles really fast.

"Um guys...?" said Chris.

"What?" asked Cimber.

"The Taliban's are not lasting very long..." Chris replied.

"Shit..." said Cimber.

He continued to watch, when a black Dragon flew down and grabbed the Taliban's armored tank, sinking its claws in it and picked it up taking it very high into the sky. The Dragon took the Taliban tank really high then dropped it. The tank fell to the ground and exploded on impact. Everyone in the U.S.A tank heard the explosion.

"What just exploded…?" asked CJ.

"Um… the Taliban's tank…" said Chris.

"Oh don't tell me that…" replied CJ.

As the Demons continued to destroy the Taliban forces Hell Hounds worked tearing a hole in the back of the group's tank.

"Hell hounds!" yelled Travis.

"Where?" asked Chris.

"At the back of the tank!" Travis replied.

CJ and Cimber looked at the back of the tank from the inside, as they could hear the scratching and tearing of the metal.

"GET THEM OFF!" yelled Chris.

"I'M TRYING!" yelled Travis.

The tank all of a sudden powered off.

"What just happened?" asked CJ.

"The Hell Hounds must have torn through something important…" said Chris.

Suddenly the Hell Hounds finally tore through the back of the tank. Chris crawled out of the gun and saw a Hell Hound head poking into the back of the tank a.

"SHIT!" yelled Chris.

Travis crawled down from the turret.

"OH DAMN!" yelled Travis.

"KILL IT!" screamed CJ.

Chris took out his sword and cut off the Hell Hounds head. Suddenly a small Demon about two feet tall crawled through the hole of the tank.

"What the hell is that?" said Travis.

"It's an Imp, kill it!" said Chris.

The Imp Jumped up on Travis and sunk its teeth into his neck then tore out a piece of Travis's neck. Travis quickly grabbed the Imp and threw it on the floor of the tank and Chris took his sword and cut its head off.

"OH MY GOD TRAVIS!" yelled CJ.

Travis dropped to the ground holding the right side of his neck with blood running down his chest and arm. Chris ran up to Travis and squatted down in front of him and looked at him.

"Dude... I don't know what we are going to do..." Chris said to Travis.

"Get my bag..." Travis said.

Chris handed Travis his back pack, Travis opened it and pulled out a bomb.

"Holly hell Travis..." said Chris.

"All of a sudden the black Dragon latched onto the side of the tank. Everyone watched as the tank shook and his teeth sunk into it coming through the inside of the tank.

"WHAT IS THAT?" yelled CJ.

The Tank began to creek; the Dragon then pulled and ripped the tank in half, right down the middle. Everyone stood on the side of the tank that still remained on the ground.

"RUN!" yelled Travis as he activated the bomb.

Cimber, CJ and Chris ran out of the torn side of the tank.

"We half to find cover! Follow me!" yelled Chris.

The Dragon dropped the other half of the tank from its mouth, the tank half crashed to the ground as the Dragon reached for Travis and grabbed his legs with its mouth. Travis let out a painful scream as the Dragons teeth sunk into his waist.

Chris lead CJ and Cimber to a flipped over truck from the Taliban's that got slaughtered by the Demons. They quickly took cover behind it, and the bomb went off. It exploded and killed the black Dragon and a few Demons around it. But most of them survived the fire. Chris looked over after the blast had cleared and saw the fiery red light peering through the jungle.

"Over there! There is the Hell Hole!" yelled Chris.

They darted out from behind the flipped over truck and took off towards the Hell Hole.

"It's almost dawn!" yelled Cimber.

Cimber ran at the back of the group and Chris leading in the front. They continued to run towards the Hell Hole when a Demon ran close behind Cimber and swung its barbed tail at Cimber and impaled her in the stomach. Cimber screamed and Chris and CJ turned around and looked.

"NO!" Chris yelled.

The Demon lifted Cimber up with its tail and then grabbed her and latched its teeth into her right shoulder and bit it off along with her collar bone. Chris pulled out his shotgun and ran up to the Demon and blew its head off. The demons body dropped to the ground and disintegrated, the sun then came up.

Chris ran up to Cimber, and dropped to his knees, picked her up and held her against his body. She looked deeply into his eyes.

"I love you Cimber! I love you baby!" Chris screamed as he began to tear up.

CJ stood there watching and crying. Cimber lifted up her hand and gently stroked the side of his face and began to speak...

"Baby... I... love... you... t-" She then died before she could finish.

Chris held her tight.

"BABY! NO!" he cried.

CJ walked up to Chris and put her hand on his shoulder.

"Come on Chris we got to finish," said CJ.

"I want to give her a funeral... she wants to be cremated..." He said.

"Ok we will cremate her," said CJ.

CHAPTER 13 –

Call in the air strike and let's go home!... or

not...

Chris and CJ stacked up a big bundle of sticks and longs. Chris placed Cimbers body on top of it. CJ took her tinder box out of her bag and lit the bundle on fire. Chris stood there and cried but tried hard to hold it in as he watched Cimber's body burn. CJ walked over and wrapped her arms around Chris. They sat there for three hours till the fire burned out. After the fire had burned Chris watched the ashes blow away into the wind.

"Come on Chris, let's find that Hell Hole," said CJ.

They walked through the jungle and finally came to the Hell Hole. Fiery red light peered out of it, along with screams and howls from down below.

"It smells like fire and rotting flesh…" said CJ.

"That's the smell of hell…" said Chris.

"It's so hot…" said CJ as she whipped the sweat from her neck.

"That's because its hell…" said Chris. "Let's close this bitch."

Chris pulled out his airstrike radio from his pocket. It was just like a cell phone but it only had two buttons. Chris pushed the button that had the symbol of a microphone on it. A voice came on:

"This is General Patten."

"General Patten this is Chris."

"What's the position soldier?" General Patten asked.

"Four hundred degrees north and ninety degrees south, sixty meters," Chris answered.

"An air strike will be there in thirty minutes, and pick up will be there in two hours, get three miles away from the area," said General Patten.

"Yes sir," replied Chris.

"When you see the helicopter, fire a flair gun," General Patten replied.

"Yes sir," said Chris.

General Patten hung up and Chris looked at CJ.

"We have thirty minutes to get three miles out of the area...." Chris said to her.

"Let's go now..." replied CJ.

"Run west!" yelled Chris.

They began to run and after twenty-eight minutes they came to a cliff that hung over the ocean.

"We got to jump!" said Chris.

"No!" yelled CJ.

Just then the jets came from beyond the horizon, flew over the island really quick and dropped the bombs.

"Too bad!" said Chris as he picked up CJ and Jumped off the cliff into the water with her in his arms.

The bombs hit the ground, exploded and closed the Hell Hole. Chris and CJ then swam to shore. When they finally got ashore they crawled up onto the beach and laid there.

"We did it..." said CJ.

"Hell yea we did..." replied Chris.

CJ got up and crawled on top of Chris and began to kiss him. He wrapped his arms around her, placing his left hand on her lower back and his right hand on her upper back and kissed her deeply.

"We have two hours till the helicopter gets her," Chris said.

CJ went back to kissing him and they began to make love on the beach as the gentle waves rolled up around them.

After an hour they finished and sat on the beach telling each other of their life and what they did. Chris then looked into CJ's eyes and she cuddled up into him.

"I love you CJ," Chris said.

She smiled and replied. "I love you too Chris."

Chris looked up and saw the helicopter in the distance

beyond the ocean.

"The helicopter!" Chris said.

CJ took out the flair gun from her bag and fired it up into the air.

The helicopter arrived, landed on the beach and General Patten got out. He walked up to Chris and CJ and shook both of their hands.

"Good work soldiers!" said General Patten.

"Thank you sir," said Chris.

"Are there any other's left alive?" the General asked.

"No sir it's just us," replied Chris.

"Ok then let's get you two home!" the General replied.

They boarded the helicopter and CJ sat next to Chris and Cuddled up tight. The helicopter took off and flew into the distance beyond the ocean. Chris looked at General Patten.

"Sir?" Chris asked.

"Yes soldier?" General Patten replied.

"How did this Hell Hole open? I've never seen that happen before," said Chris.

The General looked at him.

"Well you have a right to know soldier. The military group that was on the island was drilling a water well to obtain fresh water from the island. And while they were drilling they went too far down and opened Hell up. Everyone on the island was killed before the location could be reported," said the General.

"That's scary," said CJ.

"Yes it is," the General replied.

"But no more worries it has been taken care of," said Chris.

"Thanks to you two soldier's," the General replied. "Let's get CJ back home first."

Chris held her tight.

"I'm going to miss you," Chris said to her.

"I'm going to miss you to," she said as she curled up close.

After eleven hours the sun had set and they have reached Indiana.

"Good lord..." said General Patten as he stood up and walked towards the helicopter opening and looked out it.

Chris and CJ got up and looked out with him.

"Where are we?" asked CJ.

"We are over Franklin, Indiana," the General replied.

They looked out and saw the town below. The town was on fire and looked abandon. No cars where moving or no people on the streets. CJ ran over to the Para shoot's and grabbed one. She put it on and jumped out the helicopter.

"CJ!" yelled Chris.

Chris ran over, grabbed a Para shoot as well, and strapped it on. General Patten grabbed Chris's arm before he jumped out after CJ.

"Good luck soldier, you know what to do, be careful," the General said.

"Yes sir," Chris replied.

The General let go of Chris's arm then he jumped out of the helicopter after CJ.

CJ pulled her Para shoot as she got close to the ground, it opened and she gently floated down to the ground. She landed close to her house by the entrance to the college she lived by. She took off her Para shoot and ran off down the street, running to her house to make sure her mom and step dad were ok. Chris landed shortly after

CJ did, took off his Para shoot then took off after her.

"CJ!" Chris yelled as he chased her down the street.

CJ finally got to her house and tried to open the door… It was locked…. She kicked down the door and ran in.

"MOM!" she yelled. "MOM!" she continued.

She got no response…. She ran into her parent's bedroom and found them. Her mom and her step dad lay in their bed half eaten… dead. CJ ran over to her mom, stroked the side of her face, laid her head on her mom's chest and began to cry. Chris walked into the house and found CJ lying on her dead mother's chest. He walked up to her and pulled her off.

"Baby… come on…" Chris said.

"NO!" she cried.

"MOM NO! MOM I LOVE YOU!" she continued.

Chris pulled her off, took her and walked her outside the house and stood in the ally with her wrapped in his arms.

"Baby I'm so sorry…" he said as he hugged her.

She held onto him like there was no tomorrow. All of a sudden they heard snarling noises begin to come from the one way street behind them. CJ turned around and looked, she saw a Demon standing there growling at them. CJ grabbed the handle of Chris's sword and pulled it out of the sword case. She let go of Chris and charged after the Demon with his sword.

"FUCK YOU!" she yelled as she charged after it.

She approached it then swung the sword at it. The Demon dodged her strike and knocked her down by jumping on top of her. She took the sword and struck off its head.

"Baby!" Chris yelled as he ran to her. "You half to be careful…" He said as he helped her up.

She looked over his shoulder and saw another Demon behind Chris, she got up and charged off after it. She swung at the Demon and the Demon blocked her hit and struck at her. She jumped back and dodged the Demons hit. She swung again and struck the Demon in the neck but didn't completely decapitate it. It swung at her again and she blocked its lashing claws with the sword. She took a second swing and this time decapitated it. The Demons body fell to the ground and turned to ash. CJ stood there breathing heavily with a sense of accomplishment. She looked over at Chris who was standing where he picked her up, looking at her. He smiled at her… Her eyes then widened as she looked beyond him and saw a blond girl standing behind him on the one way street.

"Destiny!" CJ yelled at the girl.

"What?" Chris said looking at her with confusion.

Chris turned around to look and when he did the girl turned around before he could see her face, and ran down the street.

"DESTINY!" CJ yelled as she began to chase her.

Chris followed CJ.

"Baby wait!" Chris yelled.

"DESTINY!" CJ continued to call as she chased the girl.

The girl then ran around a corner and lost them.

"Destiny?" CJ said as she ran around the corner and didn't see her.

Chris caught up to CJ, took his sword from her hand and put it back into its case.

"Baby please…" he said to her.

He looked to his left and saw a auto repair shop for cars.

"CJ… baby… Come on we need to make you a sword," Chris

said.

She grabbed his hand and he led her into the auto shop. Chris looked around and found a blow torch.

"I need a knife," Chris said to her.

"I have this extra one," said CJ as she pulled out a knife with brass knuckles on the handle.

"Perfect!" he said as he grabbed it from her.

He took the cutting torch and cut off the blade of the knife.

"What are you doing to my knife?" asked CJ.

"Making you a sword," Chris replied. "Besides you have another one latched to your right calf."

He took the cutting torch and walked up to a piece of scrap metal against the left wall. He took the torch and cut out a sword in the scrap metal. He then attached the perfectly cut blade to the handle of the knife and then sharpened the blade with a grinder. After words he began to create a sword case from the side of a broken car door. CJ quickly took the sword and ran outside.

"CJ!" yelled Chris. "I half to finish your sword case!"

She ran down to the town square and saw Demons crawling

all over the square. All of the Demons approached her. Six of them stood there surrounding her. The first one charged her... She took her sword and swung at it, hit it and cut off its head. Then the next one charged her and she struck its head off as well...

Chris finished the sword case and ran outside with it, running after CJ. He came to the square and saw CJ standing there with one last Demon to fight. It charged her and jumped up in the air at her with its mouth open for her face. She ducked down and swung her sword above her and cut the Demon in half. The Demons half's of the body laid on the ground screaming and moving. CJ walked up to it and cut the head off both half's and the Demons half's disintegrated.

"Damn..." Chris said as he looked at her. "Here is your sword case babe."

He handed it to her and she threw it on over her back and put the sword in its sword case.

Chapter 14 — Destiny

CJ looked back behind her and saw the blond girl standing there looking at the ground.

"Destiny!" CJ yelled and started to run towards her.

"Baby the sun in almost up," Chris said.

The blond girl then began to run again. CJ chased and yelled for her continuously.

"Destiny wait!" CJ yelled.

The girl then ran behind a building and the sun finally rose. CJ ran behind the building with Chris following right behind her. When they came around the building the girl sat there on the ground with her back towards them.

"Who is Destiny?" Chris asked CJ.

"She's my best friend." CJ replied.

CJ approached the girl and put her hand on her shoulder.

"Destiny...?" CJ said.

The girl then turned around and looked at CJ.

"CJ...." She said.

"Oh my god Destiny!" CJ said as she wrapped her arms around her and hugged her.

"Chris this is Destiny my best friend. Destiny this is Chris my boyfriend." said CJ.

CJ held Destiny forward and looked at her.

"Destiny?" CJ asked as she looked into Destiny's eyes.

"What?" Destiny replied.

"What's wrong with your eyes...?" CJ said as she continued to look into them.

"What do you mean?" Destiny asked.

Chris looked at her and saw that color of her eyes were red.

"You... you have green eyes..." said CJ.

"Yea and?" Destiny asked.

"Their red…" said CJ.

"I'm sick…" said Destiny.

"Destiny you're going to come with us…" said CJ.

"Ok," Destiny replied.

Chris walked over to a car that had a headless body in the driver's side seat and a broken window with blood on the glass. He opened the door and threw out the body. CJ walked Destiny over to the car and put her in the back seat. She then walked over to the passenger side and got in. Chris got in and started up the car and shut the door.

"I need food…" Chris said looking at CJ.

"Me too…" CJ replied. "There is a grocery store up here on the highway."

"Alright then that's where we will go," said Chris.

They drove up to the grocery store and walked inside.

"The food section is over there," said CJ as she pointed.

Chris walked over in the direction that CJ pointed and found the meet section. Chris and CJ began to grab food that they wanted to eat. They found a spot on the floor, sat down to eat and began to open their food.

"Sit down Destiny," said CJ.

Destiny sat down beside her and looked at what she was eating.

"You hungry?" CJ asked.

Destiny shook her head.

"She doesn't talk much," said Chris.

"Yea I noticed... This is not like her," CJ replied.

Destiny looked up at CJ.

"The night after..." She said.

"The night after?" asked CJ.

"It's been four days now... since it happened," Destiny said.

"What are you talking about?" asked CJ.

"The night after you left... I went to Rae's house because I was worried about you. You got recruited at school during soccer... I was supposed to go to your house... so I went to Rae's. We were watching TV when it came on the news that creature's where destroying the place… then it happened… me and Rae began to hear the noises… the screaming and howling of them… They busted threw the window and took Rae… they killed her… Then they came after me…" Destiny stopped talking.

"Then what happened?" asked CJ.

"I don't remember… a Demon hit me then I blacked out…" Destiny said.

CJ hugged Destiny and teard up a bit from Rae's death.

"Hun I'm so sorry," CJ said.

Destiny wrapped her arms around her and cried.

"She said we were gone for four days… I thought time went faster on the island…?" Chris said.

"It does… It only lasted seven hours…" replied CJ. "Time must have gone faster on the island…."

"No… The hell hole must have caused it to happen…" said Chris.

"Yea…" said CJ. "But night time was the same… it lasted eight hours…"

"The Hell Hole caused day to go by faster so the Demons could be out more often…" Chris said.

"Damn…" said CJ.

Destiny looked behind Chris and quickly looked down at the ground.

"What?" said Chris.

Suddenly a shot gun barrel was placed on the back of Chris's head.

Chris slowly stood up.

"Lookie hear," A voice from behind him said.

CJ looked at the person behind Chris and saw it was a kid from her school that she saw before.

"Who are you?" said Chris.

"I'm known as a raider," the boy said. "And this is the raider's grocery store you're trespassing in."

Then another one walked up beside him. It was a female. CJ looked at her and realized she's seen her in school too. Destiny looked up real quick and took a glimpse of the raiders. The female raider looked at Destiny and saw her eyes.

"Hey! She one of them!" yelled the raider as she pointed her gun at Destiny.

"Kill her!" said the male raider.

Chris turned around quickly and grabbed the shot gun from the male raider's hand. He took it and shot the raider in the chest. Then CJ pulled out her pistol and shot the female raider.

"What did they mean you're one of them?" asked CJ.

Destiny looked up at her.

"I'm... I'm a survivor?" she said to CJ.

"Why are they killing you because you're a survivor?" Chris asked.

"They kill anyone who is not another raider," Destiny replied.

"Destiny... let's get you some medicine..." said CJ.

She walked Destiny over to the medicine section. When they got there CJ grabbed some medicine off the shelf and gave it to Destiny.

"Here take this," CJ said.

Destiny grabbed the pills and put them in her mouth then swallowed without water.

"Let's get out of here..." said Chris.

"Good idea," replied CJ.

After they got out of the store they reached the parking lot. And when they did a Demon stood their staring at them.

"What the hell...?" said CJ.

"Holy shit... It's out in day light..." said Chris.

The Demon charged them and Chris quickly took out his whip and swung it at the Demon and cut off its head. The Demons body fell to the ground and turned to ash.

"That was weird and scary..." said CJ.

They walked to their car and got in.

"We half to find this Hell Hole..." said Chris as he started up the car and began to drive off.

"Where did the Demons start coming from when the news reported it Destiny?" Chris asked her.

"Indy City..." Destiny said.

"The Hell Hole is in Indy then..." said CJ. "But why... why the hell was it out in sunlight?"

"At first... they only came out at night... but now they come out in the day..." Destiny said. "The more human blood and flesh they consume... the more they can do…"

"So… they evolve…" said Chris.

"They never did that on the island…" said CJ.

"It makes sense though." said Chris. "On the island there weren't many people to consume. They only got fed when people where put on the island. So no food means no way to evolve… they don't eat to live. They eat to evolve…"

"Yea… there in a city now… it's an all you can eat buffet." said CJ.

"Fuck…" said Chris as he continued to drive the car down the road. "What way to Indy?" Chris asked.

"Keep on this road" said CJ. "It will take us through greenwood and you can get on the highway into Indy from there."

"Ok," said Chris.

They continued down the road for two miles when their path was blocked right outside of greenwood.

"Oh my god…" said Chris.

CJ's eyes widened as she looked at this huge Demon standing as tall as a three story building on the road. It was massive and ripped with muscles and had wings as big as its body and a long lashing tail, coming out the sides of its head was two very long horns on both sides of his head. The Demon held a light pole in his hand that he had pulled out of the ground to use as a weapon. Destiny darted out the side of the car and ran for cover. Chris and CJ got out and readied their self to fight it.

"We could use one of Travis's grenades right now..." said CJ. "How are we going to kill it...?" CJ asked Chris.

"Cut off its head..." Chris replied.

"Yea and how are we going to do that...?" CJ asked franticly as the Demon approached them.

"We will find a way..." Chris replied.

Just then an armored car pulled up behind the Demon and four raiders got out. One had a RPG launcher. He fired the RPG at the Demon, hit it in the back of the head and blew the back of its head off. The Demon let out a loud scream then turned around, swinging the light pole at the raiders. It hit the one raider along with the raider's car. The raider flew to the ground and died and the car rolled over and crushed the raider with the RPG. Two raiders remained. While the Demon had its back turned to Chris and CJ while it was finishing off the last two raiders, Chris took his sword and knife out and ran up to the Demon. He jumped up and drove his sword and knife into the Demons back. He began to climb his way up the Demons back with the sword and knife, driving them into the Demons back. The Demon dropped the light pole then reached its hands around its back and tried to grab Chris. Chris took his sword and slashed the Demons right hand. The Demon pulled its hand away and held it with its other hand and let out a loud scream.

Chris finally reached the Demons head. When he got up there he noticed there was no hole in the back of its head where the rocket had hit. He put up his knife and held on with his left hand to his sword that was still in the Demons shoulder. The Demon began to reach its hand around its back reaching for Chris again. Chris quickly took out his whip and slung it around the Demons neck; the blade of the whip came around to the back of the Demons neck and stuck deep into it. Chris pulled the whip as tight as he could and the blade began to sink in the neck of the Demon. The Demon quickly grabbed at the chain of the whip around its neck, but before it could the whip had cut deep into the Demons neck. The Demon began to sink its claws into its own neck trying to tear out the whip. Chris pulled tighter and tighter win finally the chain came all the way through the Demons neck, the Demons head fell off its shoulder's, onto the ground and disintegrated. Chris grabbed the sword still stuck in the Demons shoulder tight. The Demons body fell forward to the ground and disintegrated. Chris fell through the body as it disintegrated, and fell straight into the ashes. Chris stood up and whipped the ashes off him. He looked over at CJ and saw a Demon running up behind her. CJ stood their smiling at Chris with no idea a Demon was behind her.

"WOO! GOOD JOB BABY!" CJ yelled as she clapped.

"CJ LOOK OUT!" screamed Chris as he pointed behind her.

Before CJ could turn around, the Demon slashed its claws and hit her in the back, knocking her to the ground.

"NO!" Chris screamed as he ran towards her.

The Demon stood there and readied its claws to impale CJ while she lay on the ground with three six inch long claw marks on her back. Chris took out his shot gun, ran up to the Demon and swung the shotgun blade at the Demons arm as it swung down at CJ. Chris

cut off the arm of the Demon and it let out a scream. The Demons

hand fell to the ground and disintegrated. Chris readied the shot gun

and aimed it at the Demons head. Before he fired the Demon raised

up its handless arm. Chris looked at the arm and noticed something

strange. The Demons hand began to regenerate back on.

"Holy shit..." said Chris.

He fired the shot gun and blew off the Demons head before the

hand finished regenerating. The Demons body fell to the ground and

turned to ash. Chris grabbed CJ, picked her up then carried her to the

car and laid her in the passenger seat. Chris got in the car and started

it up.

"Destiny get in the car!" Chris yelled to her.

She ran over and got in the back seat of the car.

"Oh my god what happened to CJ?" Destiny asked.

"A Demon got her," Chris replied.

"Where is the hospital at?" Chris asked.

"I'll show you," Destiny replied.

Chris followed Destiny's directions and after forty minutes

finally came to the hospital, back in Franklin.

"It's not too far from the town square…" said Chris.

"Yea…" replied Destiny.

Chris picked up CJ and took her into the hospital.

"We got to stich that up baby…" he said to CJ. "Destiny wait out here and keep watch"

"Ok" replied Destiny.

Chris took her into one of the hospital rooms; he grabbed the sutures and a bottle of betadine to clean the cut.

"This might hurt a bit baby…" he said as he began to poor the betadine on her cuts.

CJ clinched her fist and let out a slight moan from the pain.

"Ok baby, I'm going to stitch you up so hold tight," said Chris.

"Ok baby," CJ replied.

He began to stich her up.

"They are evolving so fast…" said Chris to.

"Why you say that?" asked CJ.

"Because I cut off the Demons hand that hit you… and it grew back…" said Chris. "And the big Demon… when I got to the top of it…

The hole in its head from the rocket was gone… it must have grown back… Their regenerating…"

"Wow… well isn't that grate?" said CJ sarcastically.

Chris finished her stiches after twenty minutes. Suddenly the intercom system came on and a voice begins to speak.

"Hey guys! I found the talky thing, and I saw a raider in here so run…"

The intercom shut off.

"What the hell… now they know we are here Destiny…" said CJ.

Chris and CJ took out their pistols. CJ had duel wield pistols, both pistols were Beretta M9's that she wore around her waist. They walked into the waiting room and a raider was crouched behind the nurses' station. He poked up from behind the desk with a mini Uzi and opened fire on CJ and Chris. They quickly took cover… The raider grabbed a radio he had on him, pushed a button on the side and began to talk in it.

"Guys we got survivors in the hospital! He said."

The radio replied back.

"Ok Cirrus we are ten minutes away from the hospital. We will be there." The voice replied.

Chris aimed his gun at the nurse's station and the raider popped his head up to fire another Uzi round on CJ and Chris. Chris quickly aimed at the raider and fired the gun. He shot the raider right in between the eyes. The raider fell to the ground dead.

"You got him baby!" said CJ.

Then they heard the toilet flush in the bath room of the waiting room. They looked over at the bathroom door and aimed their guns at it. The door opened and Destiny walked out.

"Destiny?" asked CJ.

"Man I had to pee so bad..." replied Destiny.

All of a sudden they heard a car pull up in the parking lot outside.

"Oh shit..." replied Destiny as she shut the bathroom door and locked it. "I'll be in here if you need me!"

"There's backup…" said Chris.

Chris and CJ walked outside, an armored expedition sat in the parking lot and eight people got out of it.

"Wow that's allot of people…" said CJ.

"I've killed more," said Chris.

The eighth guy got out of the car.

"What the hell… Look at that freak…" said Chris.

A big guy got out of the car that stood seven/nine foot tall.

"He's huge…" said CJ.

He then pulled a mini gun out of the car.

"He's got a mini gun, for the love of god…" said Chris.

"He's covered in metal…" said CJ.

"He's armored…" said Chris.

The guy with the mini gun began to open fire… Chris and CJ ducked behind the pillars of the hospital entrance.

"OH MY GOD!" said CJ as she put her hands over her head.

"BABY!" yelled Chris.

"WHAT?" CJ replied.

"I GOT A PLAN!" he said.

The bullets from the mini gone continued to fly by them as they hid behind the columns.

"A PLAN?" she replied.

"YEA, YOU DISTRACT THEM AND I'LL TAKE CARE OF THE REST!" Chris yelled.

"DISTRACT THEM?! ARE YOU KIDDING ME?!" CJ replied.

"NO BABY! YOU CAN DO IT, TRUST ME!" Chris said.

"OK BABY!" said CJ.

"AT LEAST TRY TO KILL A FEW!" said Chris.

"NO PROBLEM..." said CJ.

"AND MAKE SURE YOU TAKE COVER!" said Chris.

"SURE..." said CJ.

The guy with the mini gun ran out of ammo and walked back to the car to grab some more.

"GO!" yelled Chris.

Chris and CJ ran out from behind the columns. Chris went right and CJ went left. Four fired at Chris and three fired at CJ. Chris took out his pistol and ran for the back of the driver's side of the car. CJ shot one guy in the head and another in the stomach with her duel pistols. Chris then began to open fire at the gas tank cap of the car. The guy with the mini gun got his gun reloaded and began to open fire on CJ, she quickly took cover. Chris then finally hit the gas cap, and the car blew up. Chris jumped for cover behind a car as the expedition exploded. The explosion took out every raider, and the guy with the mini gun fell to the ground.

Chris walked over to CJ.

"Baby are you okay?" he asked.

"Yea... I'm amazed that I'm alive..." she replied.

"Of course you are, you kick ass!" he said as he smiled at her.

Chris then began to hear growling behind him.

"Oh shit..." he said to himself.

CJ's eyes widened, Chris turned around and looked.

"Holy hell that is a huge Hell Hound..." Chris said as he looked at the Hell Hound standing there, that was twice the size of a normal one. The Hell Hound stood five feet tall.

"Their getting bigger..." said CJ.

"Their evolving so fast..." Chris said.

The guy with the mini gun then stood up.

"This guy is still alive!" yelled CJ.

"I don't care about him... I care about this huge ass Hell Hound..." said Chris.

A Demon then came up behind the huge guy with the mini gun as he readied and aimed his gun at Chris and CJ. The Demon behind him stood four inches taller than the enormous guy. The Demon opened its mouth and bit off the guy's head, Right through the armor and bone. The guy's body fell to the ground and the Demon continued to eat it.

"See why I wasn't scared of that guy now...?" said Chris.

The Hell Hound then lunged at Chris, Chris drew his sword and ducked down swinging his sword above him and cut the Hell Hound in half. The two half's of the Hell Hound fell to the ground, but did not disintegrate... They then began to regenerate.

"No, no, no..." said Chris as he watched.

"This is insane..." said CJ.

The body half's finished regenerating and now two giant Hell Hounds stood there growling, ready to kill them.

"You get one and I get the other..." Chris said to CJ.

CJ put up her pistols and drew her sword. The Hell Hounds then ran at them. Chris jumped out of the way of his and cut off the head. The one on CJ then jumped on her, knocking her on the ground. It stood over her trying to bite off her face. Chris took his sword and swung it at the Hell Hounds neck and cut its head off. The body then fell down and disintegrated.

The Demon that was eating the body of the big raider then stopped eating it and came after Chris. Chris took of his whip and quickly lashed off the Demons head. As the Demons body fell and disintegrated. A red Dragon flew through the sky and landed in the parking lot in front of Chris and CJ.

"OH MY GOD!" said CJ as Chris helped her up. "What are we going do now?" she asked.

The Dragon reared its head back and opened its mouth; it got ready to blow fire. Chris took CJ's hand and ran with her back behind the pillars as the Dragon let out its fire at them. They took cover behind the hospital columns when the Dragon took its tail and knocked them down. Chris and CJ jumped out of the way of the hospital entrance as it collapsed from lack of support since the columns where knocked down. Chris quickly took out his whip.

"Stay safe baby!" he said to CJ.

"Be careful baby!" she said to him.

Chris ran up to the Dragon, swung his whip at the Dragon and struck it in the face, right across its left eye. The Dragon let out a roar and swung its left arm at Chris. The Dragon hit Chris and he flew against the side of the hospital wall.

"Ouch..." Chris said as he slowly got back up.

The Dragon opened its mouth and lunged its open mouth at Chris ready to eat him. Chris quickly jumped out of way and the Dragon bit into the side of the building. Chris then took his whip and swung at the Dragons neck and cut its head off. The body and the head of the Dragon disintegrated into ash.

Chris ran over to CJ and she quickly rapped her arms around him.

"Come on baby, let's get Destiny and head to Indy." Chris said to CJ.

They walked into the hospital waiting room and knocked on

the bathroom door.

"Destiny! Let's go!" said CJ.

Destiny opened the door.

"Are they gone?" asked Destiny.

"Yea they are Destiny, let's go..." CJ said.

They walked out to the parking lot and got in their car. As they got in the car the sun was almost set... They drove down the road to the stoplight at a four way intersection ready to turn left to head to Indy when Destiny opened the right side passenger car door and bolted out the car down the road. Chris immediately stopped the car.

"Where is she going?" asked Chris.

"I don't know..." said CJ.

CJ got out of the car and chased her down the street.

"Destiny!" CJ yelled.

Destiny continued to run till the sun finally went down. CJ had chased her all the way back to the town square. Destiny sat in front of a gas station on the street by the town square, Destiny was bent over holding her face and quivering. CJ walked over to Destiny and Chris came shortly behind CJ. CJ put her hands on Destiny's back.

"Destiny?" CJ asked her.

Destiny then stood up and held her head to the sky and began to scream. Chris and CJ watched helplessly.

"DESTINY?" yelled CJ.

Destiny's eye's then began to change. They turned pure red and her teeth began to turn sharp.

"Destiny, talk to me..." said CJ.

Destiny turned around and swung her right arm at CJ and hit her. CJ flew twenty feet away and hit the ground.

"SUFFER!" Destiny yelled.

CJ slowly got back up.

"SHE'S POSSESSED!" yelled Chris.

Destiny then ran after Chris. Chris quickly kicked Destiny when she approached him. Destiny flew back ten feet and hit the ground. Chris drew his sword, walked up to her, swung his sword at Destiny and stabbed her in the stomach. Destiny got up, grabbed the sword that was impaled through her, and pulled it out. She dropped the sword on the ground, grabbed Chris's throat and lifted him in the air. She then opened her mouth and threw up blood all over him.

Chris took his knife out and stabbed Destiny in the head. Destiny threw Chris and screamed. Chris flew, hit a car that was near and fell on the ground. Destiny took the knife out of her head and walked up to Chris ready to stab him with the knife. She then grabbed Chris again and picked him up by the throat, reared back her right arm with the knife in her hand; ready to lung it into his head. CJ walked up behind Destiny.

"Kill her baby... It's the only way..." Chris said as he grabbed Destiny's right arm as she lunged the knife towards him.

CJ took her sword out and readied to swing it.

"I'm sorry Destiny..." said CJ as she then swung the sword.

The sword struck off Destiny's head. Destiny then dropped Chris as her body and head fell to the ground. When her body fell down, a red misty substance began to come out of Destiny's neck. The mist then began to take form.

"The Demon..." said Chris.

The Demon finally took form from the mist and stood there standing eight feet tall, staring at Chris and CJ. CJ then swung her sword at the Demon and the Demon blocked her hit with its right arm and threw CJ. Chris then swung his sword and the Demon blocked his hit with his left arm and threw Chis. Chris and CJ fell to the ground then quickly back got up. The Demon did not charge them; it stood there and stared at them. It then began to speak.

"For too long... The human race has been the dominant species... You live in God's protection no more... you invited us in your world... Now we will have control... salvation is reserved for no one... now you will all die..." The Demon said.

It then charged CJ; she quickly took her sword and struck off its head. The Demons body fell to the ground and disintegrated.

"That must be the final stage of evolving..." said Chris.

"Talking?" asked CJ.

"No... Possessing..." said Chris.

"What did it mean by we invited them?" CJ asked.

"It must have been when the first Hell Hole was opened up by accident... They were able to get to earth... now they are trying to take over..." said Chris.

"We half to take out this Hell Hole..." said CJ.

"I agree, but first I need to sleep..." said Chis. "I haven't slept since the first night on the island."

"We can go to my house," said CJ.

"Ok," said Chris.

They got in the car and headed to CJ's house.

Chapter 15 — Closing Time

They arrived at CJs house.

"Baby let me go in first…" said Chris.

"Ok baby," CJ replied.

Chris walked in and closed the door to her parent's room. CJ then walked in and began to tear up.

"Baby it's ok," said Chris as he wrapped his arms around her and held her tight.

Chris shut the house door and locked it.

"I need to shower," said Chris. "I'm covered in blood and ashes…"

CJ showed him the bathroom and Chris walked in and started to undress. CJ shut the door and stood in there and watched.

"What?" Chris asked her.

"I'm going to shower with you," she said to him as she began to take off her shirt.

Forty-five minutes later they finished showering and got dressed, then walked into CJ's bedroom and laid on the bed. CJ then began to Chris kiss passionately. Chris wrapped his arms around her, laid on top of her; they took each other's clothes off and began to make love.

After they finished making love they got back in their underwear and got ready to sleep. CJ was wrapped tight in Chris's arms.

"I'll keep you safe baby," Chris said as he held her tight.

She cuddled up close to Chris's chest.

"I love you," Chris said to her.

She looked up at him and smiled brightly.

"I love you too," CJ replied.

They cuddled up tight under the covers and went to sleep.

Twenty-three hours later CJ woke up.

"Baby…" CJ said as she shook Chris's shoulder.

Chris woke up.

"Huh? What is it baby?" Chris asked her.

She pointed at her bed room window. Chris looked out and saw the sun setting.

"Wow… how long were we asleep?" Chris asked.

"Like twenty something hours…" CJ said.

"Wow…Well I certainly feel rested," said Chris.

"Yea…" said CJ.

She kissed him on the lips.

"Let's go kick ass baby!" said CJ. "We got a hell hole to close."

Chris and CJ got armored back up and Chris put back on his war paint with the black lipstick he still had from the Taliban soldier.

"I want some!" said CJ.

"Ok baby," said Chris as he smiled at her.

He drew dark black circles around her eyes and colored them in.

"Now you're all painted up!" said Chris.

She kissed him and they headed out the door and got in the car.

"Let's go kick some ass tonight," said Chris as he started up the car.

He started up the car and headed towards Greenwood. They drove for an hour when they finally came to Green wood and reached the Greenwood mall. As soon as they got there a raider car approached them. The raider in the passenger side of the car pulled a RPG out the window and fired it.

"Jump out of the car!" yelled Chris.

Chris and CJ opened their door and dove out of the car. The rocket hit the car and it blew up. The impact of the blast threw Chris and CJ and knocked Chris and CJ out.

"Go check them!" yelled one of the raiders.

Two raiders got out of the car and one walked over to CJ and the other walked over to Chris.

"This one is knocked out!" said the raider standing over Chris.

"So is this one!" yelled the raider standing over CJ.

"Well pack them up and we will take them to the boss!" yelled the raider driver.

They loaded Chris and CJ up into the car and took them into the mall.

Chris woke up to the sound of CJ's yelling at a raider.

"Let us go so I can kick your ass!" yelled CJ.

"Where are we...?" asked Chris as he awoke.

"You're in the Greenwood mall... men's clothing department. We armored it up good and wired it with electricity to keep Demons out. The mall is made with stone anyways so it's hard for the Demons to bite through it," said a raider who was surrounded by other raiders, one on his left and one on his right.

"Where are the clothes?" asked Chris.

"We cleaned them out," said the raider.

"Who are you?" asked Chris.

"I am the leader of the raiders... I am Commander Zack," he said to them.

Chris looked to his right and saw a table with his and CJ's weapons on it along with his hat. Chris quickly devised a plan to get Zack to try to attack him and somehow cut the ropes.

"Well commander Zack... Go to Hell, you ugly piece of shit," said Chris.

"Now I'm going to slit your throat..." Commander Zack said as he pulled out a knife and walked towards Chris.

"NO! BABY!" yelled CJ.

Zack swung the knife at Chris, Chris quickly pulled forward and fell to the ground on the chair face first, and Zack's knife hit the ropes on Chris's hands, cutting them off. Chris quickly got up, punched Zack in the face and knocked him to the ground.

"Kill him!" yelled Zack.

Chris ran over to the table with his weapons on it as the raiders fired at him, grabbed the pistol and took two shots shooting both the raiders that guarded Zack. Zack stood up and pulled out a Desert Eagle pistol and before he could fire Chris shot him in the head.

"That was my last shot..." Chris said to CJ.

"Untie me!" CJ said.

Chris grabbed his knife, walked over to CJ and cut the ropes.

"Thanks babe," said CJ as she stood up and hugged him.

"Let's get equipped babe," said Chris.

They walked over to the table and put their weapons back on, Chris put his hat back on. CJ put back on her duel pistols and her sword, along with her combat knife. Chris put back on his whip, sword, knife, shotgun, and pistol.

"It's going to be a fight to get out of there," said Chris.

"Yea..." said CJ.

They opened the door and walked out into the mall. Ten raiders stood between them and the door that exited the mall.

"Let's do this," said Chris as he pulled out his shot gun and pumped it.

The fight with the raiders began... Chris fired his shot gun at the first one that he came close to as the raider fired at him, and blew his head off. He then swung his sword on the bottom of his shotgun at the other raider and cut his throat.

CJ took out her duel pistols and began to shoot the raiders. She fired four shots, two out of both guns. She shot three raiders and missed one. The raider continued to open fire on CJ and Chris. CJ fired again and finally got the other raider she missed.

A raider then opened fire on Chris with an AK-47; Chris took cover behind a mall map. He then took out his whip and jumped out from behind the mall map, swung his whip at the raider with the AK-47 and cut his head off.

CJ fired two of her last shots and got one more raider but missed the other.

Chris took his shot gun, fired on the next raider and got him in the chest from ten feet away.

CJ then took out her sword and charged the last raider and stabbed him through the chest. The raider fell to the ground dead.

"Wow you got more kills then me this time baby," said Chris

smiling at CJ.

"Oh you're counting now?" CJ asked as she smiled at him.

"Maybe," said Chris smiling back at her.

"Look at the food department," said CJ pointing at a wooden sign above the food apartment.

It read "Armory" painted on the wooden sign hanging above the food department.

Chris and CJ ran in there and loaded up on ammo.

"Thank God! I needed more!" said CJ.

"Same here!" said Chris.

They finished loading up and getting extra ammo then started to walk out when Chris saw a RPG hanging on the wall.

"I got an Idea," said Chris as he grabbed it.

"Let's go," CJ said.

They walked out to the entrance to the mall.

"Wait!" said Chris before CJ walked out it.

Chris ran over to the mall map and looked for another way

out. He saw that the raiders drew on the map where there were entrances that they blocked. He also saw that they drew their garage for their armored vehicles on the map.

"That's where we will go!" said Chris.

"Ok... But what's going on?" asked CJ.

"I'm going to blow up this wall and let the Demons in to slaughter the raiders," said Chris.

"Oh shit..." said CJ.

"You're going to need your pistols to shoot raiders on the way to the garage," said Chris.

CJ pulled out her pistols and got ready; Chris then fired at the wall and blew a hole into it. The damage to the electric fence around the armored wall caused it to shut off. Demons then began to poor into the mall. Chris dropped the empty RPG and ran, with CJ following him.

They ran down to the garage shooting raider's that tried to stop them on the way. The Demons chasing them would stop and devour the raiders that got shot, or killed the ones that Chris and CJ did not shoot.

As they approached the garage, Chris kicked open the door to the vehicle garage and Chris and CJ quickly ran in.

"Get in that eighteen wheeler!" yelled Chris.

CJ got into the passenger side of the semi; Chris got in the driver's side and started it up.

"Here is a garage door remote!" said CJ as she grabbed it off the dashboard.

She clicked it... the garage door opened and Chris drove the armored semi out, running over the Demons in his path.

"Fallow this road to the highway," CJ said to Chris.

Chris got on the road and fallowed it for thirty-five minutes before he finally got the highway. After another thirty-five minutes they saw Indy approaching in the distance.

"Oh my god it looks horrible..." said CJ.

The city of Indianapolis sat in ruins, on fire with flying demons and dragons in the air around it.

After twenty minutes they finally came to a sign that said "Welcome to Indianapolis"

"The city is crawling with Demons," said Chris.

"There seems to be more of them in the direction of the airport," CJ said.

"Then that's where we will go… to the airport," said Chris.

He followed the highway by the sign that said "Indianapolis international airport"

"Look over there! That bright red light!" said CJ as she pointed to the runway of the airport.

Chris looked over and saw a fiery red light coming out of the ground of the runway.

"That's the Hell Hole!" said Chris.

Chris veered off the highway and drove through the fence that went around the airport. He began to run through the wave of Demons in-between them and the Hell Hole.

They finally got to the Hell Hole and Chris stopped beside it.

"Don't stop!" yelled CJ as Demons began to crawl on the trailer less semi-truck and tear it apart. Chris quickly grabbed the small radio that connected to General Patten, He pushed the talk button on it and General Patten's voice came through.

    "Report soldier," the General said.

    "Five hundred meters south three thousand meters east!" yelled Chris.

    "We will be there in twenty minutes, Get three miles out of the area; we will pick you up where you were dropped off at," said General Patten.

    The call ended.

    Chris put his foot on the gas pedal and took off. The semi plowed through the Demons and the ones crawling on it fell off one at a time.

    After twenty minutes they reached the welcome to Indianapolis sign again.

    "We made it!" yelled CJ.

The Jets flew over the area and then dropped the bombs. CJ looked in the passenger mirror and saw the mushroom cloud in the distance.

"We made it..." said CJ.

"Yes we did" said Chris.

Chris looked at the sky and saw the sun coming up. CJ laid her head down on Chris's lap and let out a sigh of relief. Chris placed his hand on her back and gently stroked it.

"Let's go home baby," he said to her.

After an hour they reached the sign that said Franklin exit. After they got off the exit ramp they saw the helicopter sitting there in hotel parking lot. Chris stopped the semi and Chris and CJ got out, they walked up to the general, he reached out and shook Chris's hand.

"Well done soldier," General Patten said.

"Sir there is some day time Demons that will still be alive," said Chris.

"We will take care of them soldier," the General said.

"Oh and there is some hostiles called raiders that have taken over the town of Franklin and Greenwood that I know of, you will know one when you see one sir," Chris Said.

"We will take care of them too, no worries soldier. Now let's get you two home," said General Patten.

"My home is gone... this was my home," said CJ.

Chris looked at her.

"You can come live with me in Texas if you would like," said Chris.

CJ looked at him and smiled.

"I'd love too," CJ replied with joy. "But I need to get to my house and pack and take care of a few things."

"We will take you there," said the General.

"Alright," said CJ.

"Get in the copter and tell us where your house is," the General said.

They loaded up and whet to CJ's house, they landed in the college parking lot a block away from CJ's house.

CJ and Chris walked into her house and CJ packed her things. After she finished packing she grabbed a picture off the dining room wall of her mom and step dad.

"Baby I need to do one last thing," CJ said to Chris.

"Ok baby," he replied.

"Take my bags and go to the helicopter please," she asked.

"Ok baby," said Chris.

Chris walked outside the house and headed to the helicopter... CJ walked outside to the tool shed and grabbed a can of gas. She then walked back into the kitchen and found a lighter in one of the kitchen drawers. She walked into her parent's room and began to tear up when she saw her mom and step dad lying there in the bed. CJ took the gas and poured it all over them and the bed. Afterword's she took the remaining gas and poured it all over the house.

"Rest in peace Mom and dad," she said as she lit the lighter.

She threw the lighter on the ground and shut the door. She cried as the inside of the house lit fire.

CJ walked back to the helicopter and saw Chris waiting there for her with her bags packed in the helicopter. She immediately ran up to him and hugged him tight. Chris looked at her, took his hand and dried up her tears.

"Come on baby, I'll take care of you now," he said to her.

She smiled and hugged him tight.

"I love you so much," said CJ as she held him tight.

"I love you too," Chris replied.

They loaded up into the helicopter and it took off. Chris and CJ sat down and strapped in tight.

"Chris and CJ you are the best and bravest damn soldiers I have ever had," the General said.

"Thank you sir," Chris and CJ replied.

As they took off Chris looked out the helicopter and saw the helicopters headed to Indy, filled with soldiers to clean up the remaining Demons and raiders.

The helicopter flew off into the distance and after four hours they arrived in Austin, Texas. The helicopter landed on the street of the housing division, in front of Chris and Cimbers house. Chris and the General unpacked CJ's bags and walked them up to the front door.

"I'll be heading back to base now," General Patten said.

"Thank you sir," said Chris and CJ.

"The pleasure was mine," he said to them. "We will send your checks in the mail."

"Thank you sir," said Chris. "If you need me again you know where to find me sir."

"I thank you for the offer soldier, you take care of your self's now," said General Patten.

"Yes sir," said Chris and CJ.

General Patten loaded up into the helicopter and took of back to Arizona.

Chris unlocked the door of the house and took in CJ's stuff. CJ walked in behind him.

"We will take down all the pictures of me and Cimber..." said

Chris as he began to tear up.

"Don't worry about it right now," said CJ as she shut the door.

She held into the bed room with Chris and then held him tight when he put down her baggage. Chris fell on the bed with her in his arms and she buried her face in his chest. She then let out a sigh of happiness, looked up at Chris and smiled.

"I'm home," CJ said.

Art and story done by Chris Schulze

Editor: Chris Schulze and Chaney Stansbury

Real Characters - Chris C. Schulze as Chris and Chaney J. Stansbury as CJ.

And Destiny Marlene as Destiny.

About the Author

Hello I'm Chris. First of all I want to say thanks for reading my book. And if you haven't read my book and you're just browsing through the book store and opened it to the end to read it this… then read my book you jerk! Ha-ha.

This is my first published book, but the second book I have ever written. My first book is called "The 3 Plagues" It is not published. It's about three legendary knights who ended up turning bad, and the leader of the three knights "Me" try's to get his girlfriend "CJ" to join him.

I'm interested in Demons and Angels, love to Draw I mostly draw Demons and Angels but I do draw other things, I love to Skateboard and spend most of my time doing stuff with my girlfriend CJ. I also love music (who doesn't) I listen to Dubstep, Metal, Heavy Metal, Alternative, Speed Metal, Death Metal, Black Metal, any kinds of Metal. I think I named them all.

This book has three real Characters in it. And Chaney Stanbury "CJ" is my girlfriend in real life, and Destiny is her really her best friend. I've been with CJ for a wonderfully long time and I've enjoyed every second of every day of our relationship.

I grew up in the small town of Burnet, Texas. And I was born in Austin, Texas, June 21st, 1991. I now live in Franklin, Indiana with my beautiful girlfriend CJ. I have four older half-sisters; Dawn Werner, Heather Drosche, Monica Burton and Natalie Hargis. The youngest one of my half-sisters is at least twenty years older than me. I also have a younger brother who is three years younger than me.

I am going to college to be a Mortician and Funeral Director, and also to be a Game Designer as a side job.

Depending on how well people liked this book will tell me if I should right another one or Continue Demo, I have loads of ideas for add-on's and continuing book's for Demo, and plenty of other ideas for new books.

Thanks for Reading my book and I hoped you enjoyed it.

www.ingramcontent.com/pod-product-compliance
Lightning Source LLC
Chambersburg PA
CBHW052145170626
46812CB00004B/1595